HONEY BUNCH:
JUST A LITTLE GIRL

BY

HELEN LOUISE THORNDYKE

Author of "Honey Bunch: Her First Visit
to the City," "Honey Bunch: Her
First Days on the Farm"

NEW YORK
GROSSET & DUNLAP
PUBLISHERS

Made in the United States of America

CONTENTS

HONEY BUNCH:
JUST A LITTLE GIRL

CHAPTER I

A BUSY MONDAY MORNING

"I HOPE this doesn't shrink," said Honey Bunch, holding up her doll's petticoat for Mrs. Miller to see. "Somehow my child's clothes shrink every time I starch 'em."

Mrs. Miller laughed. Her round, red face shone through a cloud of steam, for she was washing. She had two large tubs filled with water and a basket of clothes stood on the floor beside her. She was rubbing a white sailor blouse up and down on the washboard and the soapsuds came up to her elbows. The sailor blouse belonged to Honey Bunch.

Honey Bunch was washing, too. She had a basin all to herself, and a chair to hold it and a cake of soap. She was washing a petticoat and a dress that belonged to Eleanor, her doll.

"Clothes get very dirty, don't they?" said Honey Bunch, holding Eleanor's petticoat up to the light as she had seen Mrs. Miller do. "I just can't seem to get the dirt out. Eleanor is such a careless child!"

Mrs. Miller walked over to the tin boiler that stood on the laundry stove and stirred the clothes in it with a long stick. Honey Bunch knew that Mrs. Miller boiled the clothes to make them clean and white. She often said so.

"I wonder if I hadn't better cook Eleanor's petticoat?" asked Honey Bunch. "I'd like her to have a nice clean petticoat and dress this week."

"You let 'em soak, Honey Bunch," said Mrs. Miller, stirring the clothes in the boiler carefully. "Let them soak in the warm water awhile; that loosens the dirt."

"All right, I will," replied Honey Bunch. "But won't it make the buttons loose, too?"

"My land, Honey Bunch, what won't you think of!" cried Mrs. Miller, putting the lid of the boiler on again and going back to her tub. "I never heard of buttons soaking loose, and I guess anything I never heard of, in connection with washing clothes, never happened!"

Honey Bunch was sure Mrs. Miller was right. The washerwoman had washed for the little girl's mother ever since Honey Bunch could remember. She was a very large washerwoman, large and jolly and good-natured. When she walked across the kitchen floor the pans in the closet rattled on their hooks. Down in the laundry there were no pans to rattle, but you always knew when Mrs. Miller was coming down the stairs, for she made each step creak and groan. But that, as Honey Bunch's daddy said, was much better than if Mrs. Miller had creaked and groaned. She never did. She was always laughing.

"There now, my wash has to soak," said Honey Bunch, who could no more work without talking than Mrs. Miller could wash without soap. "Lady Clare, have you anything you'd like me to wash for you?"

Lady Clare opened her lazy green eyes and stared at Honey Bunch. Lady Clare was a beautiful, sleek cat and she was dressed in black velvet with an ermine collar. That was the reason she was called Lady Clare. Honey Bunch had not noticed at first that the cat wore black velvet; Daddy had pointed out that to her. Daddy had shown her the collar of white ermine that went right around the kitty-cat's throat, too. Some people said Lady Clare had black fur and was striped with white fur around her neck, but Honey Bunch knew better; it was black velvet and ermine as plain as plain could be.

"I might wash Lady Clare," said Honey Bunch, leaning over her basin of clothes to stroke the cat.

"Well, I wouldn't, if I were you," advised Mrs. Miller, beginning to put a lunch cloth through the wringer. "In the first place, a cat just naturally hates to be washed. In the second place, her fur might run."

"Run?" said Honey Bunch, in great surprise. "Where would it run to?"

Mrs. Miller laughed so hard she had to wipe her eyes on her blue and white gingham apron.

"I declare, Honey Bunch, you're the oddest young one I ever knew!" she told the little girl. "I don't mean the kind of running your legs and feet do. You recollect how the blue silk embroidery in your pongee blouse all ran into the collar when I washed it, don't you? That's the kind of 'run' I'm talking about."

"Oh!" said Honey Bunch, who remembered the pongee blouse very well. "Would Lady Clare's black fur run into her white fur if I washed her?"

"I'm not saying it would," answered Mrs. Miller. "You never can tell. Cats aren't made to be washed with soap and water."

"Then I won't wash you, Lady Clare," said Honey Bunch. "But the little poodle dog across the street has a bath every Saturday afternoon."

"Poodle dogs are different," declared the wise Mrs. Miller. "I've heard folks say they put bluing in the water for a white poodle dog,

the same as if he was a sheet or a tablecloth.
It makes 'em white."

"I guess they don't put them through the
wringer, though," said Honey Bunch, and
Mrs. Miller agreed that she had never known
of a poodle dog whose bath included a turn
through the wringer.

"You'd better be rinsing out Eleanor's
clothes, if you want me to hang them up when
I take the next basket out," said the washerwoman kindly.

Lady Clare, sure that soapsuds and water
were not for her, curled up close to Honey
Bunch's feet and went to sleep, while Honey
Bunch herself went to work so seriously that
she quite forgot to talk. Her small pink
tongue, just the tip of it, showed between her
little white teeth. Honey Bunch was determined to make a good job of her rinsing.

She was such a little girl, this Honey Bunch,
that the lowest chair in the laundry made her a
table. You see she wasn't quite five years
old, so, of course, she couldn't be tall. And
while her real name was not Honey Bunch, a

great many people who loved her dearly said
it ought to be.

"'Bunch of Sweetness,' is too long to say
every day," her daddy had declared. "So let's
call her 'Honey Bunch.'"

And by and by every one except Daddy and
Mother had almost forgotten that Gertrude
Marion Morton was the little girl's real name,
for Honey Bunch seemed to suit her so exactly. That kind of name would not have
done at all for a cross little girl, or for one
that liked to tease, or even for a little girl who
meant to be good but who often forgot.
Honey Bunch was so sunny and smiling and
so sweet, every day, that the name just fitted
her.

Daddy Morton was a lawyer. He went
often to a place called a "court" where it was
very solemn and serious and quiet and where
most important things happened. Honey
Bunch had never been to court, but Mother
Morton had. She had heard Daddy make
long speeches there, and when Honey Bunch
was older, she said, perhaps she might some

day go to court and hear Daddy speak, too.

Honey Bunch did not wash every Monday morning, though Mrs. Miller did. Indeed, Mrs. Miller washed nearly every day in the week for somebody. This particular bright and sunny Monday morning, Mother Morton had given Honey Bunch a little basin and had told her she might wash her doll's clothes while Mrs. Miller was in the laundry. Honey Bunch liked to wash. Indeed she liked to do a great many things. She was always busy and happy.

"I could turn the wringer for you," said Honey Bunch, when she had finished rinsing the petticoat and white pique dress that belonged to Eleanor. "Wouldn't you like to have some help, Mrs. Miller?"

"You couldn't turn the wringer, thank you just the same," replied Mrs. Miller politely. "First place, it's too high for you, and then again it turns too stiff. I think it needs a mite of oil, but I'll wait till I'm through this Monday. Are you all through washing, Honey Bunch?"

"I haven't anything else to wash," explained Honey Bunch.

"My goodness, what about your doll's stockings?" asked Mrs. Miller. "They have to be washed last thing, you know. I'm sure Eleanor would like to have a clean pair of stockings—don't you think she would?"

"Oh, yes, I know she would," cried Honey Bunch, delighted with the idea. "But she hasn't any others."

Honey Bunch meant the doll had no other stockings to wear while those she had on were being washed, but Mrs. Miller said such tiny stockings would dry quickly and if Honey Bunch thought Eleanor might take cold, the doll's feet could be wrapped in the old knitted muffler that hung on the laundry door.

Honey Bunch took down the muffler and wrapped Eleanor in it and then she put the stockings in the basin of water and "jiggled" them up and down to let the warm, soapy water run through them.

"I'm glad I didn't wash Lady Clare," she

cried in a moment. "Look how the black comes out!"

Sure enough, the water was black from the doll's little stockings and Mrs. Miller said it was the dye.

"Who dyed them?" asked Honey Bunch.

"The folks that manufactured them," said Mrs. Miller, lifting the lid from the boiler and letting out great clouds of steam. "Most everything we wear is dyed, Honey Bunch."

"Is this dress dyed?" said Honey Bunch, looking down at the green chambray frock she wore.

"Yes, that's dyed," answered Mrs. Miller, lifting, with the long stick, the boiled clothes from the boiler into a tub of clear rinsing water. "Stand away from this steam, child; you don't want to get burned."

"Will the dye come out of my dress?" asked Honey Bunch anxiously.

She was very fond of her green dress and she didn't want the pretty color to come out.

"I'll see that it doesn't," promised Mrs.

Miller. "When I get that dress to wash I'll set the color first."

Honey Bunch wanted to ask how she "set the color" in a dress, but before she could ask the question, another thought popped into her head; why not "set the color" in her doll's stockings?

"Look, Mrs. Miller!" she called excitedly. "Look——" and Honey Bunch leaned across the chair which held her basin of water to get the tiny stockings which she had hung on a nail in the wall.

Her elbow struck the edge of the basin, it tilted, splash! over went the basin and the water on the sleeping Lady Clare! The poor cat sprang up with a howl and a spzz-t! and, rushing across the laundry, dashed between the feet of Mrs. Miller, who had her back to Honey Bunch, and on out through the open door into the yard.

"My land, has that cat got a fit?" gasped Mrs. Miller. "Did she bite you, Honey Bunch? She looks mad enough to scratch my eyes out!"

Mrs. Miller hurried to the door to look at Lady Clare and Honey Bunch peeped around her. The cat sat in the center of the yard, glaring at the house. Lady Clare's velvet and ermine were soaking wet and her feelings were plainly hurt.

"I knocked the basin over on her," giggled Honey Bunch. "It tipped. I guess Lady Clare thought I changed my mind and meant to wash her, anyway."

The loud buzz of the electric bell sounded through the upstairs hall.

"Oh, my!" whispered Honey Bunch eagerly. "Somebody's come! I'll be back in a minute."

And she scuttled up the back stairs, intending to go to the door for Mother who she knew was busy writing letters.

CHAPTER II

DADDY'S VISITOR

WHEN Honey Bunch reached the top of the back stairs she heard voices in the parlor. Mother had already answered the doorbell. She was talking to some one.

Honey Bunch tiptoed down the hall and peeped between the green curtains. Mother was sitting in one of the chairs that stood in the bay window and a strange man was sitting opposite to her.

"Perhaps it is the carpet man," said Honey Bunch to herself.

The carpet man had come one day to measure the stairs for new carpet. Honey Bunch remembered him very well. He had carried the nicest little ruler with brass hinges, a little ruler that folded up and folded up till Honey Bunch was seriously afraid there would be no ruler left. But the carpet man said it

13

was just small enough, when he had it all folded, to go in his vest pocket and he let Honey Bunch take it and open it up and fold it together again. Honey Bunch hoped it was the carpet man who had rung the doorbell.

"But he looks different," whispered the little girl to herself. "The carpet man didn't wear glasses. This must be somebody else."

She was so anxious to find out who the caller was that she poked her yellow head further in among the green curtains and the stranger saw her.

"Hello!" he said pleasantly.

And Honey Bunch's mother saw her and smiled.

"Come in, dear," said Mother. "Mr. Subways, this is my little daughter, Gertrude."

Mr. Subways held out his hand, taking both of Honey Bunch's small hands at once.

"Now I'm sure——" he said, patting the little hands gently. "I'm as sure as can be that they do not call you Gertrude."

Honey Bunch was sometimes a bit afraid of strange people. Not exactly afraid, perhaps, but a little shy. You know how you feel when some one you have never seen before speaks to you; for a minute or two you can't remember anything to say. That was the way Honey Bunch often felt.

But Mr. Subways didn't seem strange after he had shaken hands with her. He reminded her of her daddy and of her Uncle Peter who came to see them every year. Honey Bunch decided that she liked Mr. Subways very much and when he asked her a question she answered him as though she had known him a long time.

"Tell me, truly," said Mr. Subways, "is Gertrude the only name you have?"

"I'm Honey Bunch," replied that small person at once. "Every one calls me Honey Bunch. But my really name is Gertrude Marion Morton."

"I knew it!" said Mr. Subways, smiling as though something pleased him. "I knew you had a happy name. Would you like to know my little girl's happy name?"

And Honey Bunch was so interested she

pressed closer to Mr. Subways. Mother was smiling, too, and listening.

"Have you a little girl?" asked Honey Bunch eagerly. "What is a happy name?"

Mr. Subways took off his glasses and placed them on his knee. Then he took a piece of pink cloth out of a little leather case he had in his pocket and began to polish his glasses carefully. He gave Honey Bunch the case to hold. It had a little snap that opened and closed the cover and Honey Bunch found that if she just touched the tip of her finger to the cover it would fly open.

"A happy name," said Mr. Subways, rubbing away with the pink cloth, "is the one people give you when they love you very much and you love them. My little girl's 'really' name, as you would say, is Lulu. But her mother and I call her 'Roses.'"

Honey Bunch asked why the little girl was called Roses and Mr. Subways said it was because she was as sweet and lovely as the flowers. Then he turned to Mrs. Morton.

"I'm so sorry Mr. Morton isn't at home," he said. "I had quite counted on seeing him. These cases drag out forever if something isn't done."

Honey Bunch stood quietly playing with the eyeglass case while her mother talked to the stranger. She could be a very quiet little girl when older people were busy. She never interrupted or asked questions when her mother or her daddy was talking to visitors. That was one reason why she was so often allowed to stay in the room when quite important matters were being talked over. "As still as a little mouse" Daddy told her she was, proudly.

"I'm sorry, too, Mr. Morton isn't at home," said Mrs. Morton. "Ordinarily I could reach him at his office by telephone for you. But to-day he has gone down to the State capital to take some special evidence. I do not expect him back till late to-night."

"I wish you would ask him to get in touch with me," said the stranger, putting on his glasses and drawing another leather case from

another pocket. Honey Bunch wished she
could have as many pockets in her dresses.
She would put something different in each
pocket, she thought.

"Here's my card," said Mr. Subways, busily writing something on a slip of pasteboard
with a silver pencil. "That address will
reach me, and I'm adding my 'phone number,
in case he wants to give me a ring. Your
husband knows my connection with this case,
Mrs. Morton, and I think he and I can serve
each other to mutual advantage."

Honey Bunch did not understand all these
long words, but she liked the way the man
smiled when he gave the card to her mother.
He rose to go the next moment and Honey
Bunch gave him back his little leather case.
Mrs. Morton rose, too, and Mr. Subways
shook hands with her, patted Honey Bunch on
the head, and said he meant to tell his little
girl all about her.

Mrs. Morton followed him to the door,
but Honey Bunch ran down the back stairs to
the laundry. She found Mrs. Miller just

ready to take out another basket of clothes.

"Your wash is about dry, Honey Bunch," the good-natured washerwoman told the little girl. "Are you going to iron the things to-day?"

"Well, I thought I would," answered Honey Bunch. "I told Eleanor I would give her a tea party this afternoon and Mother is coming."

"What's Mother going to do, darling?" asked Mrs. Morton, coming into the laundry, a yellow envelope in her hand.

"You said you'd come to my dolls' tea party," explained Honey Bunch. "You said you'd be lonely this afternoon, 'cause Daddy wouldn't be coming home for dinner, and you'd visit with me."

"Daddy won't be home for two or three days, dear," said Mrs. Morton. "A boy brought me this telegram while I was standing at the door talking to Mr.—Mr.—Oh, what was that man's name? Anyway, the man who wanted to see Daddy. You and I will be alone for nearly a week, Honey Bunch."

"Where's Mr. Morton going, ma'am?" asked Mrs. Miller, putting down the heavy clothes basket again, so that she might listen more comfortably.

"To Washington," said Honey Bunch's mother, pulling a sheet of yellow paper from the yellow envelope and reading it. "He says he's found it necessary to go to Washington and he's going right from Paxton. He thinks he will be able to get back home by Friday."

"Well, he's a busy man," declared Mrs. Miller, picking up her basket and moving slowly toward the door. "I s'pose he doesn't think any more of going to Washington than I do of going down to Paxton to the State Fair; and that's more traveling than I care to do as a rule, I'll say right out."

Mrs. Morton went upstairs—she said it was time to begin to think about getting lunch—and Honey Bunch trotted out into the yard after Mrs. Miller.

"Will you make my iron get hot?" she coaxed.

"Bless your heart, child, I'll fix you up in a jiffy," replied Mrs. Miller, pinning clean napkins on the line almost as fast as she talked. "Let me get this basketful pinned out and I'll see that you have everything you want."

Lady Clare was sitting on the fence, and though she opened her eyes when Honey Bunch called to her, she would not come down. Her fur was nearly dry and Mrs. Miller was sure she had forgotten all about the over-turned basin of water.

"I don't think she has," said Honey Bunch, following the washerwoman back into the house. "Do you know what I think, Mrs. Miller? I think Lady Clare is sorry it is Monday."

Mrs. Miller said "Perhaps" and bustled around to fix a place for Honey Bunch to iron her doll's clothes. She spread a piece of blanket on the table and put a clean piece of muslin over that. Then she placed a chair and helped Honey Bunch up. When the little girl kneeled down, she was just the right height to iron comfortably.

Honey Bunch had a little toy iron her daddy had brought her and Mrs. Miller heated this on the laundry stove. She didn't let it get too hot, because she said an iron that was too hot was very bad for clothes.

"There is nothing, Honey Bunch," said Mrs. Miller seriously, "that looks worse than a scorched spot on nice, clean clothes. You mustn't have your iron too hot, or you'll scorch that pretty dress you want Eleanor to wear to the tea party this afternoon."

"Maybe this is too hot," said Honey Bunch anxiously, pointing to the iron Mrs. Miller had brought to her and put on the little nickel stand.

"It isn't too hot if it doesn't burn your finger," Mrs. Miller explained. "Put your finger on the iron, Honey Bunch. Is that too hot?"

"No, it's just right," said Honey Bunch, holding her fat little finger against the tip of the tiny iron. "Just exactly right. And now I'll iron my washing all nice."

She had finished the last piece and was

climbing down from the chair when Mother
called that lunch was ready and had any one
seen a hungry little girl?

"Me!" cried Honey Bunch, running eagerly upstairs. "I'm the hungry little girl,
Mother!"

Daddy Morton seldom came home to lunch,
so it was natural for Honey Bunch and her
mother to eat without him in the pretty dining
room. As soon as she had finished her rice
pudding and Mother said she might be excused, Honey Bunch hurried up to her room
to dress her dolls and get ready for the party.

Eleanor had her clean dress to wear, of
course, and the other dolls had new ribbons
or traded hats or did something to "look like
a party," Honey Bunch said. She very often
dressed them in each other's clothes, which
certainly made them look different.

"There now, you're all fixed, and I hope
you'll be good till I come back," said Honey
Bunch, when she had the dolls dressed and
each was sitting stiffly up in a chair. "I'm
going down to invite Mother."

Honey Bunch ran downstairs and found her mother sitting in the parlor.

"How do you do," said the little girl, who knew exactly what to do, for her mother often played tea party with her. "Will you come to my dolls' tea party this afternoon?"

"I should like to come very much," replied Mrs. Morton; "but I have no dollie to bring with me."

"Then I'm afraid you'll have to bring cookies," said Honey Bunch, trying not to smile. "Have you any cookies?"

"Oh, yes, I have cookies," Mrs. Morton said. "Cookies and milk."

"I'll carry the milk pitcher," promised Honey Bunch, and then she had to laugh because Mother's eyes were twinkling so merrily.

CHAPTER III

AN AFTERNOON TEA PARTY

THE cookies and the milk were ready on the dining-room table—Mother had known she was to be invited to a tea party, you see—and Honey Bunch carried the pitcher up to her room without spilling a drop.

Honey Bunch had a pretty little room all to herself. The woodwork was white and the furniture was painted white, too. She had a low box in which she kept her toys and that was covered with a cloth material having blue and white and black figures woven in it. Some of the figures were little boys and some were little girls. Honey Bunch could tell you how many there were, for she had counted them with Mother's help. There were twenty little boys and eight little girls.

Honey Bunch had her own white bureau

and her own white bed and she was very
proud of them. But she liked best the white
goatskin rug Daddy had given her on her last
birthday. She was so fond of this rug that
whenever she gave the dolls a party she
dragged it out on the screened porch where
it would be sure to be seen.

The screened porch opened from the room
that was Honey Bunch's bedroom. It was a
small, square porch and had screens to keep
the flies out, and awnings to keep the sun off,
and long blinds to pull down when Honey
Bunch slept outdoors, as she often did on
warm nights. From this porch you could
look right into the trees, and Honey Bunch
said she thought it was as nice as the little
house her mother had had in an apple tree
when she was a little girl.

"The party's all ready," said Honey Bunch
to her mother, as they reached her room.
"The dolls are waiting for you."

Sure enough, the dolls were just as Honey
Bunch had left them; not one had jumped
down and gone to playing and mussed her

best frock. They were very good children and Honey Bunch told them so.

"The table's all set, too," said Honey Bunch, leading Mother out on the porch and showing her the little table with the blue and white china neatly in place.

The goatskin rug was under the rocker where Mother was to sit, for Honey Bunch always wanted her company to have the nicest things.

Mother sat down in the rocker and Honey Bunch put the cookies and the milk on the table. She brought out the dolls and put them all in one chair. Then it was time for the party to begin.

And at that very moment the strangest things began to happen. Honey Bunch did not think them strange; dear no, she was used to having them happen!

What were these strange things? Well, the milk, for one thing, turned into hot tea. Hot tea with cream and sugar in it, as Mother and Daddy had it every Sunday night, Honey Bunch knew. And the cookies turned into

charlotte russe cream puffs—at least that was
what Honey Bunch said they were and she
ought to know.

But stranger than this was the way Mother,
Honey Bunch's own Mother Morton, became
Mrs. Simpson. And Honey Bunch herself
was Mrs. Hatchett.

"Will you have cream and sugar in your
tea, Mrs. Simpson?" asked Honey Bunch of
Mother politely.

"Yes, thank you," answered Mother. "Do
you allow your little girls to have tea, Mrs.
Hatchett?"

Honey Bunch shook her head. She loved
to be called Mrs. Hatchett. She thought that
when she grew up she would like to be called
Mrs. Hatchett all the time.

"No, I never let any of my children drink
tea," said Honey Bunch, or Mrs. Hatchett,
as she would want us to call her. "I think
tea is bad for children. They have bread and
butter. But I wish you would try one of my
charlotte russe cream puffs, Mrs. Simpson."

Mrs. Simpson took a cookie and said it was

the best charlotte russe cream puff she had
ever eaten.

"This tea is pretty hot," declared little Mrs.
Hatchett. "But then strong, hot tea puts life
into me."

Mrs. Simpson, who was Mrs. Morton really, you know, laughed at that.

"You've heard Mrs. Miller say that, Honey
Bunch—I mean, Mrs. Hatchett," she said.
"It seems to me one of your children is missing; didn't the china doll come to the party
with us?"

"I guess she fell off the chair," said the china
doll's mother. "Yes, there she is down on the
rug. She's a careless girl. Did you know her
nose was chipped in one place, Mother? Excuse me, Mrs. Simpson?"

"Her nose broken? Why, when did the
china doll break her nose, dear?" Honey
Bunch's mother asked.

Honey Bunch poured a little more "tea"
into her blue and white cup.

"Her nose isn't broken—just chipped in one
place," she explained. "It happened to her

'cause she is so careless. She fell out of the window."

"Fell out of the window! Why, Mrs. Hatchett, how dreadful!" cried Honey Bunch's mother.

"Yes, isn't it? My dear Mrs. Simpson, you ought to have seen her fall out!" exclaimed the china doll's mother. "I put her on the window sill to dry after I'd given her a bath and then I knocked her off with my elbow."

The visitor agreed that this was very careless, and then, as all the charlotte russe cream puffs were gone and the tea pot was quite dry, Honey Bunch announced that the party was over and that she wasn't Mrs. Hatchett any more. She trotted downstairs after Mother and said good-by to Mrs. Miller, who was going home to her own family. Honey Bunch helped Mother get dinner a little later, and that night she slept with her because they both felt lonely without Daddy Morton.

They were very glad indeed to see him when Friday came. Mother was upstairs sewing and Honey Bunch was reading aloud to her. Honey Bunch couldn't read, not really read, of course, for she was not five years old. But she loved to pretend and she often took a newspaper or a book and read aloud to Mother. Honey Bunch made up the story as she went along and it was very interesting. Her mother said it was.

"The little girl went downtown," read Honey Bunch this Friday afternoon. "She thought she would buy her mother a birthday present. But all the stores were closed because it was Christopher day."

"What day, dear?" asked Mother curiously.

"Christopher day," repeated Honey Bunch, looking over the top of her book. "That's what it says, Mother."

"Are you sure it doesn't say 'Christopher Columbus Day'?" suggested Mother. "Don't you remember I told you about Christopher Columbus last week?"

Honey Bunch looked at the book again.

"Perhaps it does mean Christopher Columbus," she said. And just then she and Mother heard a little click of the hall door downstairs.

"Daddy!" shrieked Honey Bunch, dropping the book and flying out into the hall. "Daddy's come!"

The little click had been his latch key in the lock. Honey Bunch knew the sound. She rushed downstairs. Daddy stood in the hall, his heavy bag at his feet.

"Well, Honey Bunch!" he said, picking his little girl up and hugging her tightly. "Miss Daddy, dear? Where's Mother?"

Mother was just behind Honey Bunch and Daddy had them both in his arms at once for a moment. Then they all went upstairs together and Daddy unpacked his bag and told Mother about his trip and answered Honey Bunch's questions and asked what they had been doing while he had been gone.

"Did you see any little girls?" asked Honey Bunch, watching Daddy smooth out his ties.

"I saw two little girls on the train," said Daddy Morton. "Most of the time they were very good but they cried for nearly an hour once and that wasn't pleasant."

"Oh, my!" said Honey Bunch, much shocked. "Did every one see them cry? Did their mother scold them?"

"Well, no, I don't think she did," answered Daddy Morton, handing a little pile of clean handkerchiefs to Mother, who put them in his top drawer. "They had different mothers, you know; there were two little girls and two mothers."

"What made them cry?" insisted Honey Bunch.

Daddy put his bag away in the closet and said he didn't know.

"But I never cry for an hour!" said Honey Bunch. "Why didn't the mothers make them stop, Daddy?"

"Well, you see, Honey Bunch, they were pretty young," explained Daddy Morton, smiling at Mother. "I don't think they were much over four months old."

"Babies!" said Honey Bunch. "They weren't little girls, Daddy; those are babies."

"You don't tell me!" answered her daddy, pretending to be surprised. "Well, they were the only little girls I saw; I know they were little girls, because they had girl names; they were Marie and Jessie."

When Honey Bunch slipped into her seat at the table that night she found a little package there. Her daddy had brought her a present from Washington. It was a cut-out set, just the gift Honey Bunch liked best. She had her own blunt-pointed scissors and she loved to cut out things. There were several sheets in this set and Honey Bunch was so interested in looking at them that she did not hear what her daddy and mother were saying until her mother mentioned letters.

"You found your letters on the hall table, didn't you, David?" she asked.

"Yes, everything all right," Daddy Morton replied. "Has any one called, Edith?"

"Why, yes," said Honey Bunch's mother. "I meant to tell you at once, David. There was a man here to see you—he said he wanted to see you very much about some case; I think it was the Thompson case—is that right?"

"I thought it was about time they tried to get some one interested," Daddy Morton said, a little excitedly. "Who was the man, Edith—did he leave a card?"

Honey Bunch's mother jumped up from the table and went into the parlor to get the card. She was gone several minutes.

"I can't find it!" she said when she came back. "I know I put it in that little silver tray, and now it isn't there. It was such an odd name I thought I'd be sure to remember it, but I saved the card to be sure. Oh, David, I'm so sorry! Is it very important? I recall he told me he was going West, but he said you could get in touch with him."

Honey Bunch looked up from her cut-outs, surprised. Her mother sounded as though something was bothering her.

"Honey Bunch, you saw the man; you remember him, don't you, dear?" her mother said eagerly. "What was his name? You tell Daddy."

Honey Bunch shut her blue eyes tight and

tried to think. What was the name of the
man who had told her his little girl's "happy
name"? She had liked him very much.

"I don't remember his name," said Honey
Bunch slowly, opening her eyes. "But he has
a little girl and her name is Lulu."

"Honey Bunch! Do try to think!" urged
her mother. "You remember that man. You
know how he looked. He gave Mother a card
with his name on and now she has lost it.
Can't you remember what I told you his name
was?"

CHAPTER IV

A MORE EXCITING PARTY

Honey Bunch thought hard again, but she couldn't remember the strange man's name. She remembered that his little girl was called "Roses" instead of Lulu, but, as Daddy Morton said, that didn't help him much.

"Well, we won't fret over what can't be helped," he said at last. "If I could get that name I haven't a doubt it would save me considerable money and more time, which is just as valuable. You don't think the card is stuck in a book or in any of the desk drawers, do you, Edith?"

Honey Bunch's pretty mother looked ready to cry. She felt so bad about the lost card.

"I ought to have put it in a safe place," she said. "But I thought that little tray was a safe place. Mrs. Miller must have thrown out the card when she cleaned. And I don't

see how I could forget the name, anyway! I
never forget a name!"

"There, there, don't blame yourself,"
Daddy Morton told her. "Perhaps the man
has a Chinese name. Here is Honey Bunch
who can't remember it, either. I wonder how
it would do if I should advertise for a man
who has a little girl named Lulu who is called
Roses. That might fetch this mysterious
stranger back to us."

Both Honey Bunch and her mother laughed
at the idea of advertising for the stranger that
way and Daddy Morton said he was glad they
felt more cheerful. But all through the rest
of the meal, even when Mother brought in
the chocolate pudding dessert, Honey Bunch
noticed that her daddy seemed to be thinking.
He even had a little "worry frown" between
his eyes.

After she had eaten her pudding Honey
Bunch went around and sat on Daddy's
knee. She often did that and he liked it very
much.

"Maybe the man's name was Farriday,"

said Honey Bunch hopefully. Mr. Farriday
lived next door to the Mortons.

"Now stop worrying your head about the
name," ordered Daddy Morton, smiling
across the table at Honey Bunch's mother, who
was thinking with a little worry frown between her eyes, too. "Perhaps you'll remember it some day, and if you don't, there is nothing to fret about. The man will come back
to see me, if he has anything important to
say."

"Oh, David, he'll think the next move
should come from you," protested Honey
Bunch's mother. "I'm so sorry I could cry."

And at that Daddy Morton pushed back
his chair and said they wouldn't wash "any
silly dishes," but instead they would go into
the parlor and play the big talking machine
until every one felt like laughing instead of
crying.

But Mother said it was time for Honey
Bunch to be in bed, and, indeed, as a rule she
did not stay up to have dinner with Daddy
and Mother. So she kissed Daddy twice on

each ear and told him she loved him "bushels"
and trotted off upstairs, trying to remember
the strange man's name all the way up.

Daddy Morton said nothing more about the
caller and, after Mother had searched the
house from garret to cellar and even emptied
the barrel of old papers ready for the waste
paper cart, to make sure that the card was
nowhere to be found, she said nothing about
it, either. In a few days Honey Bunch had
forgotten the incident entirely.

She had other things to think about, had
Honey Bunch. There were the cut-outs, for
one thing. She spent several days cutting
them out and bending them into shape and
playing with them. And then she thought
what fun it would be to give a dolls' party
and ask the dolls who lived near to come.

"Give a dolls' party?" said Mother, when
Honey Bunch asked her. "Why, dear, I don't
see any reason why you shouldn't give a party.
How many little girls and their dolls do you
want to invite?"

So Honey Bunch counted and she found

there were seven little girls who lived on the same street—Mary and Fannie Graham, Kitty and Cora Williams, Anna Martin, Ida Camp and Grace Winters—whom she would like to ask to come to her party and bring their dolls.

Honey Bunch told Mother what to say and Mother wrote the invitations. They were written on the tiniest of note paper and when they were folded and sealed they were not much larger than two postage stamps.

"Please come to my dolls' party," read these invitations. "Bring your good doll with you. The party begins at three o'clock this afternoon."

Honey Bunch explained that she didn't want to ask the girls to bring their "best" dolls, because they might think that meant their largest and finest, the doll with the best clothes perhaps.

"I want them to bring their child who acts the best," said Honey Bunch. "Now there is Esther—I can't let her come to the party at all. She teased Eleanor and made her cry, so Esther has to stand in the corner all this afternoon and Eleanor is coming to the party."

Honey Bunch took her invitations around herself and it proved to be a very good plan because she waited while each invited guest opened and read the note—or had Honey Bunch tell her what was in the note—and said whether or not she could come. Every one of the seven asked could come, and when Honey Bunch had left the last note she hurried home to tell Mother that "all the party" would be there.

The porch looked very pretty when it was fixed for the party. The goatskin rug was there, of course; Honey Bunch had seen to that. The little round table was spread with the whitest of white cloths and the blue and white dishes were neatly arranged. There was a little vase of flowers in the center and little peanut parrots at each little girl's place. Honey Bunch's mother had made the parrots. She painted the peanuts to look like the birds' heads and then glued colored tissue paper on to make the tails. Besides the flowers and the dishes and the parrots, there were little brown bread sandwiches, and milk to drink, and a round sponge cake. Oh, no wonder the girls all smiled when they saw that pretty table.

Honey Bunch had six of her dolls ready to receive the guests before the party began. But when she had put a chair between her own chair and the one left for Ida Camp—who was her best friend—she found there would not be room enough for each doll to have a separate chair.

"I guess I'll have only one of my dolls come," she said to Mother. "Then all the dolls can sit in one chair; maybe it wouldn't be polite for me to have six children and the other girls only one."

So Eleanor, the oldest doll, was chosen to stay and the others were put away. They did not seem to mind it at all and not one pouted or frowned. I do not know of many little girls who would continue to smile if they were sent home from a party, especially after they had seen the cake and the sandwiches on the table, do you?

Promptly at three o'clock the girls came

with their dolls. Then such a busy chatter arose on the screened porch! Most of the dolls knew each other, but some had to be introduced and all their clothes had to be admired and compared. Most of the dolls were very pretty, but Cora Williams had brought a rag doll.

"She's pretty old," explained Cora, "and she never goes anywhere. I'm sure her feelings are hurt because I haven't been taking her around with me. I guess she likes to go to parties as much as any one."

"Of course she does!" agreed kind little Honey Bunch. "She can sit next to Eleanor and I hope she will have a good time."

The dolls didn't say much, but their small mothers made up for that. They talked all the time they were eating the sandwiches and drinking the milk; they chattered while they fed their dolls the crumbs of the cake—every one knows that cake crumbs are good for dolls, but that a whole piece of cake is apt to make a doll very sick. The dolls' mothers talked and laughed and ate and had a very good time indeed and so did the dolls, if their contented smiles told the truth.

"Look at that funny wagon!" cried Cora, peering under the awning as a gaily painted wagon rumbled past the house.

All the girls left the table—everything was eaten up now—and crowded around Cora to look out into the street. Honey Bunch glanced over her shoulder, into her room, and saw a little brown and white dog standing there, wagging his tail.

"Is there any cake left for me?" he seemed to say.

"Whose dog is that?" asked Honey Bunch.

"Oh, goodness, that's our dog," said Grace Winters. "He must have followed me here. I wonder who let him in. Teddy, you're a bad dog!"

Teddy wagged his tail. He thought he was a good dog to find his own way to the party.

"I suppose I'll have to take him home," grumbled Grace. "I shut the gate before I left, but he must have jumped the fence. He is always tagging me."

"Don't take him home—let him stay," said
Honey Bunch. "Does he know any tricks,
Grace?"

Grace was just opening her mouth to say,
"No," when Teddy spied something that
pleased him very much. While the girls had
been looking at the wagon, the rag doll, whose
name was Sarah Jane, had toppled out of the
chair where all the dolls sat together and had
fallen down on the goatskin rug. Teddy's
sharp eyes saw her at once, and he thought
he had found a chance for a game.

He gave a quick jump and landed on poor
Sarah Jane. Cora saw him and cried out in
alarm. "He'll kill Sarah Jane!" Cora
cried.

Teddy sunk his sharp white teeth into the
soft rag doll and shook her quickly. It was
his way of playing.

"Drop that, Teddy!" said Grace. "Drop
it. You're a bad, bad dog!"

Teddy wagged his tail and shook Sarah
Jane again. One of her leather shoes came
off, and Cora, who was sure her dear doll

would be shaken to bits, started after Teddy.
He saw her coming and turned and ran.

Downstairs Teddy fled, eight small girls
after him. Down the front stairs, through
the hall, into the parlor, out through the
dining-room, pellmell into the kitchen where
Mrs. Miller was cleaning silver, the dog
raced, the girls following him. They were
all crying, "Drop that, Teddy! Drop it,
Teddy!" and the more noise they made, the
brighter Teddy's brown eyes shone and the
firmer hold he took on the rag doll. He
thought it was great fun.

Just as he shot into the kitchen, for the
folding door was fastened back and there was
nothing to stop him, the grocery boy knocked
at the screen door in the kitchen and Mrs.
Miller opened it to let him in. This gave
Teddy his chance and he dashed out; through
the astonished grocery boy's legs, and across
the side lawn he galloped. Before the grocery boy could get his breath or find out where
the dog had come from, eight little girls rushed
past him, knocking his basket out of his hand.

Around the side of the house they ran, each
one shouting, "Drop it, Teddy! Drop it,
Teddy!"

"Is this a lunatic asylum?" asked the grocery boy of Mrs. Miller.

"Land no," she said, laughing. "Honey
Bunch is giving a dolls' tea party, that's all."

And the grocery boy said that was the first
time he ever had a dolls' tea party walk right
over him and he thought it was a queer kind
of party for any one to be giving. But of
course the grocery boy didn't know about poor
Sarah Jane.

CHAPTER V

SARAH JANE IS SAVED

TEDDY, with Sarah Jane in his mouth, had run across the side lawn and was out in the street before the little girls reached the back porch.

"There he is! I see him!" cried Honey Bunch, pointing to the dog who stood in the middle of the sidewalk before the next-door house. "Come on, we can catch him!"

But Teddy had no idea of standing still to be caught. He wagged his tail, to show the children that he was friendly, but what he wanted them to do was to chase him. As soon as Honey Bunch came running toward him, away he darted and up the street he galloped as fast as his four legs would take him. And after him, hair flying, ribbon-bows streaming, ran eight little girls as fast as their legs would carry them.

"Drop it, Teddy! Drop it!" they still
shouted, but as Teddy still ran on, in a few
moments they were too warm and out of
breath to shout any more.

"I can't run another step!" cried Grace
Winters. "Not another step! Oh, my, I'm
so hot!" And she sat down on the curbstone
and fanned herself with her handkerchief.

They all stopped. Honey Bunch's socks
had come down and were rolled in little wads
over her shoes. Cora Williams had lost the
circle comb out of her hair and the hair was
getting in her eyes. Every one had red cheeks
from running and their faces were streaked
with perspiration and dust. Altogether, they
did not look much like a tea party company.

Teddy stopped, too. He stood a little way
off, the rag doll still in his mouth. He was
panting, but he wagged his tail encouragingly.

"Come, chase me some more," he seemed
to be saying. "Come on—perhaps you'll
catch me this time."

"I should think you could get the doll away
from him," said Fannie Graham to Grace.

"He's your dog. Doesn't he ever mind you?"

"He belongs to my brother," explained Grace. " 'Sides, you can't make a dog mind when he doesn't want to; can you, Honey Bunch?"

"I don't know," said Honey Bunch. "But maybe I can make Teddy give us the doll."

All the time she had been jolting over curbs and turning up streets, you see, Honey Bunch had been thinking. And now she was quite sure she knew what to do.

"I don't believe you can get the doll away from him at all," said Grace. "If you try to snatch it he may bite you. My mother says you must never snatch anything away from a dog."

"Well, I know when the baby across the street came to see us," replied Honey Bunch slowly, "he wanted to play with the little china clock. He had it in his hands and he wouldn't put it down. His mother was going to slap him, but my mother took my little woolly lamb and held it out to him and he gave her the clock and took that."

"But Teddy isn't a baby," argued Grace.

"And he hasn't got a china clock in his mouth," giggled Fannie.

Honey Bunch looked at them. She knew exactly what she wanted to say, but she had to think as she put it into words.

"No, Teddy isn't a baby, he's a doggie," she said. "But don't you think if we gave him something else he liked, he would drop the doll?"

"He likes things to eat," Grace declared.

"All right, I'll get him a bone," said Honey Bunch. "Does he like bones, Grace?"

"He loves 'em," answered Grace, scrubbing her hands with her handkerchief and leaving the little white square very dirty indeed. "But you haven't any bone, Honey Bunch."

"I'll get one," Honey Bunch replied, staring at Teddy as though he might help her to think.

"I know where our butcher shop is on our street," she said, "but Teddy might run away if I went 'way back there. Our butcher gives the man on the corner bones for his dog, and

I guess he would give us one for Teddy. Do you want to wait while I go back and ask him?"

"No, that will take too long," said Grace. "Look, Honey Bunch, there's a butcher store down that street; maybe he will give you a bone if you ask him."

Grace meant the butcher himself, not the butcher shop, might give Honey Bunch a bone. But Honey Bunch was too excited to notice what Grace was saying.

"I wouldn't go into a strange store and ask them to give me anything," cried Mary Graham. "Don't you go, Honey Bunch."

"I don't mind," said Honey Bunch bravely. "That is, not much. I don't want Teddy to chew up Sarah Jane."

Then Ida Camp spoke up and said she would go with Honey Bunch. Ida was a little girl who was scared to pieces if a stranger spoke to her and who always blushed bright red and tried to hide behind her teacher if she was called on to recite the golden text in her Sunday school. Ida would not be much

help to Honey Bunch, when it came to asking the butcher for a bone, but it was good
of her to offer to go and it was brave, too.

"All right, you two go and we'll wait here
and not let Teddy run off," said Grace, who
was very comfortable on the curb.

Honey Bunch and Ida started down the
street to the butcher shop and Teddy lay down
on the grass, the rag doll beside him. He
thought, perhaps, that they were all resting
before they began another race.

"What are you going to say?" whispered
Ida, as she followed Honey Bunch up the
shop steps. "Oh, my, look at the people!"

There were several people in the store, buy-
ing meat, and Honey Bunch felt almost as uncomfortable as Ida when she opened the
screen door and went in.

There were two long marble counters, one
on each side of the shop, and two men back
of each counter busy cutting meat for the cus-
tomers. Far down at one end there was a boy
in a white jacket turning some kind of a machine. He had red hair and he looked kind

and jolly. Honey Bunch decided he looked like a boy who might be willing to give away a bone.

"We'll go 'way down here," Honey Bunch whispered to Ida.

The floor of the store was covered with sawdust and it was fun to scuffle through that as they walked to the end of the shop. Honey Bunch wondered why her mother didn't have sawdust in the kitchen, at least. She thought it was very nice to have on a floor and it was certainly pleasant to walk in.

The red-haired boy was waiting on a woman when the two little girls reached his end of the counter and they sat down on a soap box to wait. Back of the box Honey Bunch discovered something that made her forget her errand.

"Look, Ida!" she whispered. "A kitty—a black one!"

Sure enough, curled up in the sawdust was the fluffiest of little black kittens, and when Honey Bunch stroked him he rolled over on his back and waved four tiny white feet in the air. Honey Bunch scooped him up and hugged him tightly, while Ida stroked his head. He seemed to like to be petted, and the red-haired boy smiled when he saw Honey Bunch hold him up to her chin.

"What is his name?" asked Honey Bunch shyly.

"We call him Suet," answered the red-haired boy. " 'Cause he is so fat, you know."

Honey Bunch didn't know that suet was the pieces of fat the butcher wrapped up with the beef and mutton he sold, but she thought it was a funny name for a cat. I do myself, as far as that goes, and you probably do, too. But then it was a good name for a butcher's cat, and that makes a difference.

The red-haired boy wrapped up the chopped beef the woman had bought and which he had been cutting in the grinder, and gave her a check which told her how much to pay the butcher. Then the boy moved down to where Honey Bunch and Ida were playing with the cat.

"Well, ladies?" he said gravely.

Honey Bunch put down the cat and stood up. She knew the butcher boy was making fun of her because his eyes were laughing though his face was very solemn. Honey Bunch did not like to be laughed at.

"Have you any bones?" she said most politely.

"Bones?" repeated the red-haired butcher boy. "Well, now, what kind of bones did you want to-day? Do you want a bone to fry, or a bone for stewing? Or, if you would prefer it, we have some good roasting bones just in."

Honey Bunch felt the red coming up into her cheeks. She looked at Ida, but Ida was playing with the cat and not paying a bit of attention to her friend. Honey Bunch looked back at the red-haired boy.

"I want a dog bone," she said, her voice shaking a little.

"Well, you shall have a dog bone," said the boy, and his eyes stopped laughing. "I'll get you the best bone we have in the shop—a regular ten-center."

Oh, this was dreadful! Honey Bunch

glanced at the people standing on either side
of her, for more had come in and the store
was really crowded. Honey Bunch felt as
if every one in the shop was looking at her,
but the idea of giving up and going away
without the bone never entered her mind.
She stood up on tiptoe, so she would be a little
taller, and leaned toward the red-haired boy.

"Could I whisper to you?" she asked. "It's
private."

The butcher boy leaned his red head down
to her and Honey Bunch, still standing on tiptoe, looked at the people near her.

"Please excuse me," said the little girl politely, so that their feelings would not be hurt.

"I haven't any money," she whispered to the
butcher boy. "And I have to have the bone
to give Teddy, Grace's dog, so he will let me
have Sarah Jane, Cora Williams' rag doll.
I'll bring you the money to-morrow, if you
don't mind waiting a little bit."

That red-haired butcher boy seemed to
understand at once. He popped a bone into
a bag, said a word to one of the men at the

counter, and then, telling Honey Bunch and
Ida to "come ahead," went with them back
to the place where they had left the other
girls and the dog and doll.

"Here, you purp," said the butcher boy,
walking over to Teddy, who wagged his tail,
"what do you mean acting so—with girls, too?
I'm ashamed of you. Here's a bone for you,
and I want you to drop that doll; and don't
ever let me hear of you carrying on like this
again."

He gave Teddy the bone, picked up the
doll, which the dog did not offer to touch, and
handed Sarah Jane back to her little mother.

"You don't live around here, do you?" said
the butcher boy to Honey Bunch. "I thought
I hadn't seen you before."

"No, we live on Grove street," answered
Honey Bunch. "We all live on the same
street. And I was having a party for the dolls
when Teddy ran off with Sarah Jane. How
much is the bone, please?"

"Nothing," said the butcher boy. "Nothing at all. We give bones away every day.

Did you think up the scheme of bribing
Teddy with a bone?"

"Yes, she did," said Ida, speaking for the
first time since she had left the shop. "Honey
Bunch thinks of lots of things."

"I knew she did as soon as I saw her," the
butcher boy declared. "Well, I have to go
back now and I think Teddy will go home
with you and act peaceable. If he steals any
more dolls, you let me know, won't you?"

They promised to let him know, and he
went back to the butcher shop and the girls
walked slowly home. Just as they reached
Honey Bunch's house and were going in to
get their dolls before they went to their own
homes, quiet little Anna Martin spoke up.

"I think that was an exciting tea party,"
she said.

CHAPTER VI

LEARNING TO COOK

NOT long after the dolls' tea party, Honey Bunch made a discovery. That is, she thought it was a discovery. She had been sweeping the sidewalk with her little broom, and close up against the steps she found a slip of paper. Honey Bunch liked to sweep and she was always finding things, for a broom, you know, digs out all the corners and will not let anything hide away.

"This," said Honey Bunch to herself, smoothing out the piece of paper, "has writing on it; maybe it is the Lulu-man's card. I'll ask Mother."

Honey Bunch called the stranger, who had called to see her Daddy while he was on his Washington trip, the "Lulu-man." Neither Honey Bunch nor Mother had ever remembered his name, though Honey Bunch re-

61

membered his little girl's name was Lulu and
that he called her Roses.

Now Honey Bunch thought perhaps she
had found the card the man had left, and that,
she knew, would make both Mother and
Daddy very happy. So she left her little
broom on the side porch and ran into the
house to find Mother and ask her.

She went upstairs, where Mother had been
when Honey Bunch went out to sweep. But
no Mother was there now. Honey Bunch
looked in every room, even the sewing room,
but she found no Mother. Then she came
downstairs and peeped in every room, but
they were all empty.

Next Honey Bunch went to the kitchen.
Some one was there, some one who stood at
the table by the window, with a large apron
on, mixing something in a yellow bowl.

"Mother!" cried Honey Bunch. "I looked
all over the house for you!"

"Did you, dear?" said Mother. "I've been
right here all the time. Did you get tired
of sweeping?"

"I found something!" replied Honey Bunch proudly. "I found it on the grass right by the steps; is it the Lulu-man's card, Mother?"

Mother dried her hands on a clean towel and took the scrap of paper Honey Bunch held out to her. She held it toward the light eagerly and looked at it carefully.

"Is it the card, Mother?" asked Honey Bunch again.

"No, darling," answered Mother. "This is nothing but a piece of an old envelope that has evidently blown off some trash basket. It isn't even any name we ever heard of I'm sorry, for Daddy would be so glad to have that man's name. Can't you remember just the first part of it, Honey Bunch? Do try."

"I did," said Honey Bunch sadly. "I tried and tried."

"Yes, I know you did," Mother told her, giving her a kiss. "Daddy says we are not to bother our heads about the card any more; but I cannot help thinking of it very often and wishing I had put it away in a safer place.

But worrying won't help me make a good pie, will it, dear?"

"Are you making a pie?" asked Honey Bunch. "Oh, Mother, you said I could bake a pie some day. You truly did, Mother. Isn't this some day, Mother?"

Her mother laughed and sifted more flour into the yellow bowl.

"I suppose this is 'some day,'" she said, smiling. "Well, Honey Bunch, if you want to learn to make a pie, perhaps now is the time for you to learn. Come here and I will tie an apron on you."

Mother took down a pink apron from a hook on the pantry door and tied it around the little girl's neck. It was so long that the ends had to be pinned up twice and Honey Bunch looked like a fat little cook when she was finally fixed.

"Now you must wash your hands very carefully," said Mother. "A good cook always has clean hands."

Honey Bunch went over to the sink and washed her hands—with soap—and dried

them—with a towel—and then announced she
was ready to make a pie.

"What kind of pie shall I make, Mother?"
she asked, quite as though she could make any
kind, if she wished to.

"I'm making an apple pie," answered her
mother. "Would you like to make an apple
pie, dear?"

Honey Bunch thought she would, and she
helped Mother clear one end of the table so
that she would have room to mix and roll her
crust.

"I'll give you some of my dough, because
that is already mixed," explained Mother.
"But you may take this apple and cut it up
for your pie. And in the cupboard you will
find a little round tin that will be just the
right size for you."

Honey Bunch found the tin and then she
was ready to cut up the apple. She was not
allowed to touch the kitchen knives as a rule,
but this morning Mother gave her a little paring knife and showed her how to use it. The
knife wasn't very sharp, so there was small

danger that the little girl would cut herself,
but it was sharp enough to cut an apple if one
worked slowly. Honey Bunch thought it was
a very good knife and she worked carefully,
peeling her apple and then cutting it in four
parts, as Mother showed her.

"Those are quarters," explained Mother.
"Now take out the little pieces of core—we
don't eat those. You are doing very nicely,
Honey Bunch. I suspect you will be a great
little cook one of these days."

"Grace Winters cut herself with the carving knife," said Honey Bunch, carefully cutting out a piece of core. "Her mother told
her not to touch it and she did and she cut her
thumb."

"That's because she was naughty," said
Honey Bunch's mother seriously. "We have
to learn to use knives like any other tools. As
long as you don't touch them, unless you first
ask if you may, you won't cut yourself, Honey
Bunch. Grace's mother knew that a carving
knife isn't for little girls to handle, but poor

Grace had to find that out for herself. Is her thumb well again, dear?"

"Pretty near well," said Honey Bunch. "She has to wear a rag tied on it yet. What do I do next, Mother?"

"Goodness, next you will need a rolling pin," answered Mother. "Let me see, what shall I give you to use? I know! Wait a minute, Honey Bunch, and I'll get you something."

Mother pulled out a drawer in a table and took out a short, round stick. It did not look like the rolling pin she used; hers was of glass and much larger around than the stick.

"Is that a rolling pin?" asked Honey Bunch doubtfully.

Mother laughed a little as she wiped the stick on a white cloth.

"Well, it will make a handy rolling pin," she said. "It is a piece of a broom stick, dear, and Daddy cut it off and sandpapered it down smooth for me. I really use it to prop up that funny little window in the pantry, but it will be just the right size for you to use as a rolling pin."

Then Mother gave Honey Bunch a little lump of the pie crust (Honey Bunch called it "dough") she had mixed in the yellow bowl, and showed her how to roll it out thin on the table top. Before they rolled the crust, they sprinkled the table with flour, so the crust would not stick.

"Now you put the crust in your tin pan and cut the apples in slices and lay them in carefully," said Mother, when Honey Bunch had rolled her "dough" in a round, flat piece. "And then I'll give you some sugar and cinnamon to sprinkle on top."

Although Honey Bunch had washed her hands very carefully before she began to bake, her pie crust looked much darker than Mother's. It was gray, really, but Honey Bunch thought perhaps it would turn whiter in the oven.

"Oh! Oh!" squealed the little girl, as she tried to pull the crust from the table to put it in her pie pan. "Oh, Mother, it's breaking!"

Mother said there was a way to lift the crust without breaking it and she showed Honey Bunch how to slip a knife underneath the crust and lift it over to the pan. Then Honey Bunch had a delightful time slicing her apples with her paring knife and arranging them in layers in the pan. Honey Bunch took a long time to fix her apples and Mother had two pies ready for the oven before the little cook was ready to put on her top crust.

She thought it was great fun to sprinkle on the sugar and cinnamon and then put on the top crust "like a blanket," she said, and pinch the edges so the apples should not fall out.

"That looks like a beautiful pie!" said Mother, when Honey Bunch held it up for her to see.

"B-zzt! B-zzt!" came two short, sharp rings of the doorbell.

"Daddy!" shouted Honey Bunch, for her father always rang the bell twice.

Honey Bunch put her pie on the nearest chair and dashed for the door. Sure enough, it was Daddy, and he seemed very glad to see her, though he had left the house only a few hours ago.

"Left my keys and came up for them!" he told Mother, who had followed Honey Bunch into the hall.

"Why didn't you telephone to me and send the office boy up?" asked Honey Bunch's mother. "It would have saved you time, David."

"Oh, I had to go over to court, anyway," answered Daddy Morton. "Say, Honey Bunch, don't you want to run upstairs and get Daddy his other glasses? You'll find them on the dresser in my room."

Honey Bunch pattered upstairs, trying not to walk on her pink apron. One end had come loose while she was making the pie. She found the glasses and hurried down. Her daddy and mother were out in the kitchen. They were talking very earnestly.

"Come here, dear, and let me pin up your apron," said her mother, and Honey Bunch, handing the glasses to Daddy, went up to

Mother and turned around to have the apron pinned up again.

"I know it is early to order it, but there'll be no harm done," said Daddy Morton.

Honey Bunch's mother fixed the apron and then put her arm around her little girl.

"How many tons do you think we shall need?" she asked.

Honey Bunch knew they were talking grown-up talk. She often heard them, and she listened quietly, wondering a little about a great many things. Grown-up people, she had found, liked to talk about many different things.

"Oh, I could guess, but I won't do that," said Daddy Morton now, who could not possibly know how anxious his little daughter was to tell him what she had been doing that morning, or he would not have talked so long without giving her a chance to tell him. "I mean to see the man who built the house and lived here two winters and ask him."

"Coal will be high, Mrs. Williams said," declared Honey Bunch's mother.

They were talking about coal to keep the house warm, Honey Bunch knew then. She leaned against Mother's knee and smiled at Daddy, who was sitting in the chair by the table.

"We have to have it, though," said Daddy, smiling back at Honey Bunch. "Have to keep little girls warm and cozy when old Jack Frost comes prowling round hunting for little fingers and toes."

"Daddy!" said Honey Bunch.

"Well, sweetness, what is it?" asked her daddy. "You've been asking me a question with your blue eyes for some time. What is it, dear?"

"I don't like to bother you," said Honey Bunch. "Mother says you like to rest when you come home. But, Daddy, if you don't mind, would you get up so I can bake my pie?"

"Bake your pie?" said her daddy. "Why, go ahead, Honey Bunch, and bake it."

"I can't 'less you get up," explained Honey Bunch. "You're sitting on it, Daddy."

Daddy Morton stared at Honey Bunch as though he had not understood her.

"Sitting on your pie?" he said. "Did you say I was *sitting* on your pie?"

Honey Bunch nodded anxiously.

"Yes, you're sitting on it," she answered. "Please, Daddy, I would like to bake it now."

Daddy Morton stood up hastily. There, in the chair was what was left of the beautiful apple pie Honey Bunch had made. It was very flat indeed, flat and "squashy," Honey Bunch said, and the little girl felt like crying.

CHAPTER VII

IN THE GARDEN

"There, there, don't cry, dearie," said Mother quickly. "I have more dough and there are plenty of apples. Cooks often have to do their work over, you know. I'll help you, Honey Bunch, and you'll have another pie made and baked before you know it."

Daddy Morton felt almost as bad about the pie as his little girl did. He had to hurry back to his office, but while Mother was brushing and scraping the flour and dough off him, he put his arm around Honey Bunch and whispered that he would bring her something nice that night.

He hurried off, and then Honey Bunch and Mother set to work to make another pie, and you may be sure this second one was not left on a chair where it might be sat upon. Honey

Bunch would hardly let go of it long enough
for Mother to put it in the oven.

And when it was taken out a little later,
a beautiful brown and smelling so perfectly
delicious, well, maybe Honey Bunch wasn't
proud of her pie! Mother said she had never
seen a finer looking pie and Mother had seen
a great many pies—she had made 'most a hun-
dred herself, Honey Bunch thought.

When Daddy Morton came home to din-
ner that night, the pie was sitting at his place
and he was as pleased as though he had made
it himself. He said that now his daughter
could cook, he wasn't afraid of ever being
hungry in his own house.

"Any time Mother wants to go away for
a little vacation, we can keep house, can't we,
Honey Bunch?" said Daddy, smiling. "You'll
do the cooking and I'll sweep and dust."

That made Honey Bunch laugh, because
when Daddy swept she had noticed that a
great many things fell down. Mother had noticed it, too. Once he had swept the front
porch for her and all the plants on the rail-

ing had fallen off and some of the pots had broken.

"Here's something for the champion pie baker," said Daddy, after he had admired the pie.

He took a little parcel out of his pocket and passed it across the table to Honey Bunch. She untied the pink string and opened the paper and there was the cunningest little cooking set you ever saw. There was a little mixing board and a tiny rolling pin and a little wooden bowl to chop things in and a wooden spoon to stir them with. Honey Bunch wanted to go right out into the kitchen and use the little set, but Mother said no, it should be put away for the next baking day.

"I shall expect another pie next week," said Daddy seriously. "I hope to have all the pie I want now that I have two girls who can bake them."

And Mother and Honey Bunch promised to keep him supplied with pie and then Daddy said, if that was the case, he'd eat a second piece of the pie Honey Bunch had

made. That, of course, was a sign that it was
an extra good pie; no one ever wants a second piece of a pie that isn't extra good.
Honey Bunch knew that.

But you are not to think that Honey Bunch
made a pie every day after she learned how.
Dear no, not even Mother did that. She had
one baking day a week in summer (in winter
she baked good things twice a week), and then
Honey Bunch loved to be in the kitchen. But
other days there were just as pleasant things
to do and as nice a place as the kitchen was.
The garden, in summer, was even nicer.

Honey Bunch loved the garden. It wasn't
a very large place, but it was filled with flowers, for Mother could make things grow "just
by smiling at them," Daddy said. There was
a lawn large enough for the croquet set, there
were two trees, between which the hammock
was swung, and all the rest was flowers.

If any one had asked Honey Bunch which
were her favorite flowers, she would have answered, "Sweet peas and 'turtiums." She
meant nasturtiums. And the reason Honey

Bunch liked these flowers best was a very good reason.

"My mother lets me pick the sweet peas and the 'turtiums," she explained to Ida Camp. "The more you pick 'em, the better they grow."

This is true, and perhaps other little girls have found it out and love the pretty sweet peas and the bright-colored nasturtiums for this reason.

Honey Bunch loved all the flowers, of course, the pansies and the tall slender larkspur and all the little, low border flowers that marked the flower beds. She helped Mother keep the naughty weeds pulled and they often worked together mornings in the garden.

One morning, though, Honey Bunch felt very important. Daddy had asked her for a bouquet, and Mother had said she might pick it all herself and take as many flowers as she pleased.

"Only do not pick the yellow roses," said Mother.

The roses were Mother's favorite flowers

and she had so many that in June many people came just to see her flowers. It was not
June now and the yellow rose bush was almost
the only rose in bloom just then. No wonder
Mother wanted to save the blossoms a little
longer. Honey Bunch liked roses, but she did
not like to pick them; they pricked her, as
she said.

"I have to make a nice bouquet for my
Daddy," said Honey Bunch to a butterfly who
sat listening on a larkspur stalk.

Daddy did not often ask for flowers, so
Honey Bunch was especially eager to pick a
beautiful bouquet for him. He wanted to take
it to a little lame boy whose window he passed
every morning. He said the boy always
waved to him and that he wanted to have
something to toss up to him the next time he
passed.

"Why doesn't the little boy go and pick
flowers in his garden?" Honey Bunch asked.
"Can't lame people pick flowers?"

"The little boy has no garden," replied
Daddy Morton. "He lives in a house where

twenty other families live and there is no
yard—just a space on the roof where clothes
can be hung to dry."

"I'll get you the *nicest* flowers for the little
boy, Daddy," Honey Bunch said, her blue
eyes looking sorry for any one who had no
pretty yard.

Lady Clare followed Honey Bunch out
into the garden. She usually slept on the
fence, and Honey Bunch thought that was a
very queer place to sleep. She didn't understand how Lady Clare could be comfortable.
To tell the truth, Honey Bunch, after watching the cat one afternoon, had decided to see
how it felt to sleep on the fence, and the ex-
periment had not been a happy one.

Mother was not at home when Honey
Bunch made up her mind to sleep on the fence,
but Mrs. Miller was ironing in the laundry.
Honey Bunch took a chair from the kitchen,
carried it out to the fence and climbed up.
Lady Clare was sleeping on the narrow top
rail and Honey Bunch tried to curl up beside
her. She tucked her feet under her dress, put

her hands in her lap, closed her eyes and—
fell off!

She screamed as she felt herself going and
Mrs. Miller rushed out. So did Mrs. Perkins, who lived next door. They found poor
Honey Bunch in a little heap on the ground,
crying. Lady Clare was nowhere to be seen.

"I was trying to sleep on the fence," wept
poor Honey Bunch, as Mrs. Miller picked her
up and held her tightly in her arms. "The
fence wobbled!"

Mrs. Perkins gave her a red apple and Mrs.
Miller carried her into the house and gave
her a little saucer of the good soup that was
cooking on the back of the stove for dinner.
Honey Bunch didn't know why things to eat
made her feel better, but they did, and by the
time she had finished the soup and eaten the
apple she had almost forgotten the black and
blue spot on her elbow.

"Cats are made different from little girls,"
Mrs. Miller told her. "A cat can climb a
tree, you know, much better than we can.
Why, Honey Bunch, a cat eats mice! You

wouldn't want to eat a mouse, would you?"

And Honey Bunch said no, she wouldn't, and then she saw that she couldn't expect to do the same things Lady Clare did, because a little girl and a cat are not at all alike.

So this morning when Lady Clare followed her out into the garden and climbed up on the fence, Honey Bunch did not try to climb the fence too. Instead, she trotted down the path to the shady, cool spot near the back porch where the green ferns grew.

"I'll put ferns all around the bouquet," said Honey Bunch, talking to herself, as she often did. "And sweet peas in the middle and then 'turtiums and maybe some of the little white flowers."

The little white flowers were very sweet, but they had such a long name that Honey Bunch never tried to say it.

Up and down among the flower beds went Honey Bunch with her little, blunt-pointed scissors, and snip! snip! went the scissors. The ferns Honey Bunch spread out on the grass and as fast as she cut a flower she put it down. She knew they would keep fresh longer if laid on the cool, moist earth and not carried in her warm hands.

"Good morning, Mr. Redbreast!" said Honey Bunch politely, speaking to a fat robin who was hunting for worms under the rose bushes.

He was a *very* stout little robin, and his vest was just as red as a vest could be. His black eyes were very bright. He looked at Honey Bunch as though he wanted to say, "Good morning," too.

"Ida would dig up a worm for you, but she isn't here," said Honey Bunch. "And I would rather not, if you don't mind."

Ida Camp dug up worms for the robins to eat. She liked to turn over the earth with her little garden spade and then see the birds snatch the worms that came wriggling out. But Honey Bunch, although she did not like the wriggling worms and thought them very ugly indeed, could not dig up a worm for a robin to eat. She would have felt sorry for the worm long after he had been eaten.

Mr. Redbreast, however, seemed able to get his own worms that morning, and Honey Bunch was so interested in seeing him pull up a long worm, bracing his little body and pulling with all his might, that she quite forgot Lady Clare sunning herself on the fence. ,

Suddenly there was a flash of something black through the garden as the cat sprang down from the fence and seemed to sail across the flower beds, straight for Mr. Redbreast. With one frightened cry, the bird flew away. Lady Clare sat down, looking rather foolish.

"You're a bad, wicked cat!" scolded Honey Bunch. "Now Mr. Redbreast didn't get his breakfast. The worm went back into the hole. I should think you'd be ashamed of yourself, scaring a little bird, Lady Clare."

Lady Clare half closed her green eyes. She was sorry she had not caught the robin, but perhaps she thought she might have better luck the next time.

"I s'pose you can't help it," said Honey Bunch, more kindly. "Daddy says it is natural for you to try to catch birds. 'Scuse me,

Lady Clare, if I hurt your feelings." And
Honey Bunch stroked the cat who purred
loudly.

"Where is my bouquet?" called Daddy
Morton, coming out on the back porch with
his hat on and his brief case in one hand. He
was all ready to go down to the office. "I
thought I was to have a bunch of flowers this
morning for my little lame friend."

CHAPTER VIII

FEEDING THE BIRDS

HONEY BUNCH looked up. She waved her scissors.

"They're all cut," she cried. "Wait a minute, Daddy. They're all cut, only I have to tie them."

She stooped down and gathered up her flowers. They were beautiful and no wonder Honey Bunch felt proud. She was sure the little lame boy would like them.

"I cut the longest stems I could," she told Daddy, holding them out for him to tie with a piece of cord Mother brought him.

"They're magnificent!" said Daddy, kissing Honey Bunch. "That boy will be tickled to pieces, or I miss my guess. If he could run around, I'd take him a ball and bat instead of flowers, but I know he would rather have these. Good-by, sweetness."

Daddy Morton was half way down the
block when he heard some one calling
him.

"David!" cried Honey Bunch. "Oh, David, come back; you've forgotten your brief
case."

"Why, Honey Bunch!" Mother laughed.
"Honey Bunch! what are you calling
Daddy?"

"David," said Honey Bunch. "You call
him David. Isn't that all right?"

Daddy, who had run back, caught up his
brief case and kissed Honey Bunch again.

"If any one tries to tell what you are going
to do next," he said, dashing down the steps,
for he wanted to make the next car, "you tell
them there is no one in the world who can
do that, Honey Bunch!"

Mrs. Miller, who had come to clean, had
heard Honey Bunch call to her daddy, and
now she came out to sweep the porch, looking rather surprised.

"Little girls don't call their fathers by their
first names, Honey Bunch," she said seriously.

"Mother calls Daddy David, don't you, Mother?" asked Honey Bunch.

"Yes. But you call him Daddy, dear," said Mother.

"But you call him Daddy, too," Honey Bunch declared.

"That's all right," said Mrs. Miller, making her broom go into all the corners. "Your mother can call your father anything she wants to. But little girls don't call their fathers by their first names."

Honey Bunch sat down on the top step to think this over.

"What is Daddy's second name?" she asked in a few moments.

Mother laughed again. She had gone into the garden to look at her larkspur.

"Daddy's whole name is David Anthony Morton, Honey Bunch," she said. "But Daddy is much the nicest name he ever had; he will tell you so if you ask him. And now, dear, don't you want to feed the birds? I don't believe there are many worms this morning for them."

That reminded Honey Bunch of the worm
Mr. Redbreast had lost when Lady Clare
frightened him away and she told Mother
about that.

"Put Lady Clare down cellar for a little
while and scatter bread for the birds," said
Mother. "I like to have you begin feeding
them while it is still warm and perhaps they
will come and eat in our garden this winter."

"But Daddy says they go down South
where it doesn't snow and it's warm," said
Honey Bunch.

"Many birds do, but not all," Mother explained. "And perhaps those that go will tell
those that stay of the garden where a nice little girl scatters sweet bread crumbs for them
every day. Then, when there is snow on the
ground, you will have little feathered friends
come to see you. You would like that,
wouldn't you, Honey Bunch?"

Honey Bunch was sure she would, and she
stooped down and picked up Lady Clare and
carried her down cellar. She kissed her as

she carried her in and explained to her that
she would have to stay in the cellar just a
little while, until the birds had finished their
breakfast. Lady Clare didn't seem to mind.
She was sleepy and had had her nice breakfast. She wasn't worried about her dinner
either. She knew some one would feed her.
She would not have to go out and hunt for
something to eat as the birds did.

When Honey Bunch had put Lady Clare
in the cellar and closed the door of the stair-
way, she went into the kitchen and found
Mother had a small pan of bread all ready
for her.

"Don't birds like butter on their bread?"
the little girl asked.

"No, I don't believe they do," replied her
mother. "I never heard of any one butter-
ing bread for the birds. This winter we will
hang out pieces of suet for them; they will
like that. But they do not need it in warm
weather."

"Suet" reminded Honey Bunch of the cat
in the butcher shop and the time Teddy, the

dog, had run away with the rag doll in his mouth.

"Mother," said Honey Bunch, "isn't it funny how one thing makes you think of another thing?"

"Yes, indeed, dearie," replied her mother. "One thing makes us think of another thing and that is called remembering."

"I remember——" said Honey Bunch suddenly.

"What do you remember, darling?" Mother smiled as she asked her, for Honey Bunch stood on tiptoe as though she were reaching for the something she had remembered.

"I thought I remembered," said Honey Bunch, looking disappointed. "I almost did, Mother. I was just going to remember the name of the man who came to see us when Daddy was away."

But though Honey Bunch tried her best, she could not, as she said, "remember the remember" again. So she took the pan of bread and went out into the garden to feed the birds.

She threw the bread as Mother had shown

her, tossing it as far from her feet as she could, for birds are timid and will not come close to a person to eat unless they have learned to know that person very well.

A little sparrow came first. He stood with his head on one side, looking at a piece of bread. Then, suddenly, he snatched it and flew away.

Either the other birds saw him with the bread in his mouth, or else, as Honey Bunch thought, he was kind enough to tell them about it, for presently the garden was full of birds, pecking and chattering and some, I am sorry to say, fighting with each other for the same piece of bread. But then, I do not think their mothers were there or they would never have acted so badly.

"Hello, Honey Bunch!" called Mrs. Perkins, coming to her back door. She lived next door to Honey Bunch, you know. "What are you doing?"

"Feeding the birds," answered Honey Bunch, holding up her pan, which was empty now. "They were just as hungry!"

"Birds always are," Mrs. Perkins told her. "I wonder if you wouldn't like to feed them that box of bird seed I had left when my canary died; would you, Honey Bunch?"

"But these are sparrows and robins, and I guess there's a blue jay in the apple tree," said Honey Bunch. "How can they eat canary seed?"

"Bless you, bird seed is bird seed," replied Mrs. Perkins. "I'll get you the box, Honey Bunch, and you can have a good time scattering it around."

Mrs. Perkins went to get the bird seed and came back in a few moments with a pasteboard box nearly filled with seed. Her canary bird had died the month before and this was seed she had bought for him to eat.

"I tell you what you do, Honey Bunch," said Mrs. Perkins. "Feed the birds most of the seed, but plant a little in a bowl. It will grow quickly and you'll have something pretty for the middle of the table."

So Honey Bunch threw most of the seed to the birds. They liked it very much and pecked at it as it lay scattered on the ground for a long time. But she saved a handful and this she planted in a little flower pot that was her own.

"I won't say a single word to anybody," said Honey Bunch, pressing down the earth with both little hands. "It will be a s'prise for Mother."

For nearly a week Honey Bunch watched the little earthen pot, and by and by something feathery and green began to show. In two or three days more the green was longer and Honey Bunch carried her little pot into the house and put it on the breakfast table, right in the center where her mother always had a bowl or vase of flowers.

"Why, Honey Bunch, how pretty!" cried Mother, when she came in from the kitchen and saw the new centerpiece. "What pretty green stuff! Where did it come from?"

"I planted it," said Honey Bunch proudly.

"Is it to eat?" asked Daddy Morton anxiously. "I think it is a salad, Mother; but I never eat salad for breakfast."

"Oh, Daddy, you don't eat it!" cried
Honey Bunch, afraid her daddy would cut
the pretty green plant and put salt and
pepper on it, perhaps. "That's bird seed,
Daddy."

"Bird seed!" repeated Daddy. "Well, I
never! Where are the birds?"

"Daddy is teasing you, dear," said Honey
Bunch's mother. "I used to plant bird seed
when I was a little girl. It makes a very
pretty bit of green. Come, Daddy, eat your
cereal, and don't be asking about birds.
Honey Bunch gave that centerpiece to me—
I know exactly what it is."

Daddy Morton came home to lunch that
noon and when Honey Bunch, who had been
planting in the garden, came in to wash her
hands, she peeped into the dining room on her
way to the bathroom.

There, among the feathery green sprays of
the sprouted bird seed, sat a very small yellow
canary.

"Oh, my!" whispered Honey Bunch. "It's
a live bird! I s'pose it knew that was bird

seed. I wonder if Daddy saw it. I'll go call him!"

But some one else was watching the little yellow bird. Lady Clare, coming into the dining room from the hall, caught sight of the little creature among the green, and Lady Clare decided that the bird was surely meant for her. Before Honey Bunch knew what was happening, the cat sprang to the table and slapped her great paw squarely across the bird's body.

"Daddy! Daddy!" screamed Honey Bunch. "Oh, Daddy, come quick! Lady Clare is killing the little bird!"

Daddy and Mother came running and Honey Bunch began to cry. By the time Daddy reached her, she was sobbing as though her heart was broken.

"Honey Bunch! My dear little girl!" Daddy took her in his arms and laid his face against hers. "What is the matter, dearest?"

"The little bird—the canary!" cried Honey Bunch. "Lady Clare killed him!"

"Oh, Honey Bunch! That isn't a real

bird!" said Daddy, pulling out his lovely big handkerchief to dry her eyes. "That is a little toy bird I brought home for you. I stuck him there to surprise you. See, dear, he is only painted wood."

Honey Bunch took the bird in her hand and looked at it. It was wood, as Daddy had said.

"David," laughed Mother, "you tried to play a joke on Honey Bunch, but I think the joke has been played on you."

"No," laughed Daddy, "the joke has been played on Lady Clare. Look how silly she seems to feel."

The cat sat under the table, washing her face. She was pretending, you see, that she had caught and eaten the bird.

"I like wooden birds," said Honey Bunch, slipping down from Daddy's lap to put her bird back again in the flower pot. "Lady Clare can't scare them, can she, Mother?"

CHAPTER IX

WHEN THE COAL CAME

"There's a wagon stopping at our house," said Honey Bunch.

She was upstairs in Mother's room standing at one of the front windows. Mother was sewing and Honey Bunch was amusing her by telling her everything she saw in the street. Mother said that darning stockings wasn't much fun, but with Honey Bunch to amuse her, she thought she could darn much faster.

"What kind of wagon?" asked Mother.

She wasn't supposed to look out of the window. Honey Bunch told her everything that went past and then Mother guessed what it was.

"It's a big wagon," said Honey Bunch. "A great big wagon. And two horses. And two men. And baskets on the back."

"Dear me, perhaps it is the huckster," said
Mother. "If it is, I must go down. We need
some salad vegetables."

"No, it isn't the huckster, he has a white
horse," declared Honey Bunch. "There are
two long black things sticking out behind the
wagon, Mother. And a man's coming up
the steps."

"I'll have to go down," said Mother, rising. "Why, dear, that is the coal!" she cried
as she saw the wagon from the window.
"Coal to keep us warm this winter. That is
the first load."

Bing! went the doorbell.

Mother hurried down and Honey Bunch
trotted after her.

"Mrs. Morton?" said the man, when
Mother opened the door. "Got two tons of
coal for you. Four more loads on the way.
Mr. Jepson says you want it all put in in one
day."

"Yes, it is such a dusty job," said Honey
Bunch's mother. "Did Mr. Morton tell you
to bring chutes?"

"Yes, he told Jepson," answered the man. "We'll shoot it in for you. I'll use the hose, if you have one; that saves some dirt."

Mr. Jepson was the man from whom Daddy Morton bought his coal.

"Let me see 'em shoot the coal, Mother?" begged Honey Bunch. "I never saw any one shoot coal, Mother."

The man laughed. He had given Mrs. Morton two slips to sign and he was waiting for them.

"I guess you think I take a pistol and fire at each lump, don't you?" he said, smiling. "Well, Sister, you hang around and you'll see how we shoot coal in. Thank you, ma'am."

Honey Bunch's mother had given him the slips and she now told him where to find the hose. Honey Bunch danced out in front to watch the men work, promising Mother not to get in their way.

It was very interesting to see them. First they took the hose and turned the water on and washed the coal. Honey Bunch supposed they did this to make it clean, but she afterward decided that no amount of water could make coal clean. Daddy told her that night that the men sprayed the coal with water so the dust would not fly in thick clouds when they put it in the cellar.

"We shoot the coal with this," said the man who had rung the doorbell, when he put the hose back and took up the "long black things" Honey Bunch had noticed on the back of the wagon.

He took both black things, "coal chutes, we call 'em," he explained to the watching Honey Bunch, and put a soap box under them to hold them off the walk. The end of one rested on the pile of coal in the wagon and the end of the other just fitted into the cellar window.

Then both men stood on top of the pile of coal and shoveled. Steady streams of coal poured down the chutes and into the cellar. Honey Bunch thought that if the men's mother should come walking down the street and see them, she would send them up to the bathroom at once and tell them to wash their faces

and hands. The little girl had never seen
such black hands and faces.

Everything about the wagon was dirty;
men, horses, blankets, baskets, and shovels.
Of course, it was the coal that made things
dirty. When one of the men pulled his handkerchief from his pocket to wipe his face,
that was coal-black, too.

Every time a person came up to the coal
chute, the men would stop shoveling and the
person would stoop down and crawl under
the chute. Many went out into the street
and walked around the wagon, instead of going under the chute. Honey Bunch suggested
to the men that they stop and take the chute
apart to let people through when they came,
but the men said if they did that they would
never get all the coal put in.

"It's all right," said one of the men to
Honey Bunch. "You see these people have
to go under your coal chute now, because you
are having coal put in your cellar; but maybe
to-morrow, or next week, they'll be having
coal put in their cellars and you'll walk under

the chute on their sidewalk. That makes it even all around."

Honey Bunch had not thought of this and she told it to the next lady who came walking by. The lady had on a white hat and Honey Bunch was sure she did not like to have to stoop down and walk under the coal chute.

"When you have coal going in your cellar I'll come and walk under your chute," promised Honey Bunch, smiling such a dear little smile that the lady smiled back and said she wished she was having coal put in the next day.

By and by the wagon was empty and the men drove away. Then another wagon came up and two more men unloaded that. Honey Bunch thought they looked just like the other two men. That was because their faces were just as dark, you see. But this wagon was pulled by two white horses and the other wagon had had black horses. That is, these horses would have been white if they had not been pulling a coal wagon. Honey Bunch

wondered if horses ever had baths. She
hoped they did.

By the time this second wagon was empty,
it was noon, and Mother called Honey Bunch
in to lunch. They ate in the kitchen, for
Mother said that was the cleanest room in the
house.

"Mrs. Miller will come and make us all
tidy again to-morrow," Mrs. Morton said,
spreading a biscuit for Honey Bunch. "And
then, I suppose, as soon as we are nicely in
order, the painters will come."

Honey Bunch wasn't thinking about painters; her thoughts were with the coal wagons.

"Will there be more coal, Mother?" she
asked, biting off a little corner of the biscuit.

"Two more wagons this afternoon," replied
her mother. "And then, I hope, we sha'n't
have to have any more coal put in for a year."

After lunch Honey Bunch went out to wait
for the next coal wagon. She sat on the steps
and waited quietly. She was wondering
whether the men would let her throw a shov-

elful of coal down the long chute. She
thought it would be fun to see it slide down
through the cellar window.

As Honey Bunch sat there in the sunshine,
she saw Lady Clare come walking across the
street. Lady Clare often went walking, and
though Honey Bunch sometimes worried for
fear she would be lost, the cat always came
safely home. Now Lady Clare was stalking
toward the cellar window. The coal men had
left it open. As Honey Bunch watched her,
Lady Clare stepped inside the window, stood
still for a moment, and then jumped.

"I wonder where she went?" said Honey
Bunch aloud.

The cat did not come back and Honey
Bunch began to think about the cellar.
Where did the coal go the men put down the
long, black chute? Was it lying in a great
pile in the middle of the cellar floor? Perhaps her mother would have to walk around
it when she went to get a glass of jelly from
the cupboard in the corner. She would not
like that, Honey Bunch was sure.

"I s'pect I'd better go see," announced Honey Bunch, rising from the steps.

She trotted around the side of the house and came to the side entry door. Her mother had gone back to her sewing and Honey Bunch thought she would not tell her about the pile of coal in the middle of the cellar floor until she knew more about it herself.

Honey Bunch opened the door that led into the cellar and went carefully down the steps. There was no coal in the center of the floor, and for a few minutes the little girl thought that the men had not put it in the cellar at all. Then she saw it, black and shining, in one of the "rooms" as she had always called the bins beside the heater.

Lady Clare sat on the coal, washing her face, and the open window above her head let in sweet, cool air. Honey Bunch thought it was very nice in the cellar.

"I'll wait and see some coal come in," she told the cat.

They had not long to wait for in a few minutes the rattle of wheels was heard and a

wagon drew up at the curb outside. Some
one rang the doorbell and Honey Bunch
knew the man was giving the slips to her
mother to sign. Mrs. Morton had explained
that these slips told Mr. Jepson his coal had
reached the right house.

While Honey Bunch stared at the window
she saw the end of the iron chute come in and
then, the next moment, with an awful clatter
and racket, the coal rushed in! Honey Bunch
had not known anything could make so
much noise, and she put her hands up to her
ears.

"Lady Clare!" she cried. "Where's Lady
Clare?"

The cat was nowhere to be seen. The coal
had come pouring in where she had sat under
the window, and as Honey Bunch looked more
coal kept coming.

"She's buried underneath!" said Honey
Bunch excitedly. "Lady Clare is deep down
under all that coal!"

As soon as Honey Bunch thought of anything, she made up her mind what to do. If

Lady Clare was under that coal, she would get her out!

Honey Bunch jumped upon the pile of coal and began to dig. She had only her little hands to work with and it seemed to her that the coal came in faster than she could toss it out of the way. She worked as hard and as fast as she could, paying no attention when a piece of coal bounded on her head. She was going to get Lady Clare out before she couldn't breathe.

The stream of coal kept coming and Honey Bunch kept working. She was crying now, because she began to be afraid that Lady Clare was buried at the very bottom of the coal pile. Tears and perspiration and coal dust made great streaks across Honey Bunch's face; her soft hair was filled with dust; her hands were as black as a coal man's. She was hot and uncomfortable and most unhappy, but she would not give up.

"Honey Bunch! Honey Bunch! Why, what in the world——" cried a voice.

Honey Bunch looked up and there stood Mother on the cellar stairs.

"Lady Clare is underneath, Mother!" shouted Honey Bunch. She had to shout, because the coal made such a noise coming in. "I saw the coal go on her, but I guess I can get her out."

"My dear child! Lady Clare is asleep in the kitchen," said Mrs. Morton, coming all the way down and over to Honey Bunch so she could hear her. "Oh, dearie, how long have you been working like this?"

Honey Bunch looked at the little pile of coal she had been able to throw on to the floor. She looked at the big heap of coal in the bin, a heap which was growing larger every minute. She didn't see *how* the cat could be upstairs when she had seen the coal land on top of her, but if Mother said so, it must be true.

"I guess," said Honey Bunch slowly, sitting down on the coal heap, "I'm just a little tired."

And Mother picked her up, all dusty as she was, and kissed her and hugged her and carried her upstairs to the clean white bathroom and gave her a bath and shampooed her hair. Then she dressed her in clean clothes and gave her the money to buy a "double decker" ice-cream cone.

"For that," she said, kissing Honey Bunch as though she loved her very much, "will take the coal-dust taste out of your mouth."

And it did.

CHAPTER X

HONEY BUNCH, PAINTER

"BUT I don't see how Lady Clare got out of the coal room," said Honey Bunch.

She was eating her ice-cream cone—it was chocolate—and Lady Clare was curled up on the cushion in the rocking chair.

"Why, dear," said Mrs. Morton, "the cat jumped when the first shovelful of coal came down the chute. You thought the coal buried her out of sight, but she ran off and you never saw her go. I'm so sorry you spent all that time in the cellar and worked so hard."

"I don't mind," Honey Bunch answered. "I don't mind one bit, Mother; because, if Lady Clare had been there, I would want to dig her out. And I thought she was there, so I had to dig, anyway."

"I see," said Mother. "And now Daddy

has turned the corner and if you want to run down and meet him, you may."

Mrs. Morton had said that she supposed after the coal was put in the cellar, the painters would come. But Honey Bunch didn't pay any attention to this, so she was much surprised to hear a noise on the back porch one morning while she was eating her breakfast and to see two strange men with ropes and ladders walking about.

"Oh, my!" cried Honey Bunch in dismay. "They're from the soda fountain!"

"The soda fountain!" repeated Daddy Morton. "What makes you say that, Honey Bunch?"

"Their coats, you know," said Honey Bunch. "The soda fountain men wear 'em. And Grace Winters says a little girl ran off with one of their spoons and the man is going to every house on this block and asking if any one has his spoon."

The soda fountain Honey Bunch meant was in the drug store at the corner of the street where the Mortons lived. But, of course,

the drug store man was not going to every
house to ask for his missing spoon. Grace
Winters was a little girl who rather liked
to make up stories to astonish other children
with.

"Those are not soda fountain men, Honey
Bunch," explained Daddy Morton. "They
are the painters. We are going to have the
house painted."

"Are we?" said Honey Bunch. "Won't
that be fun!"

Her eyes sparkled and, as she had finished
breakfast, Mother said she might be excused,
so she ran out on the porch to see the painters.
They wore white overalls and jackets, so it
really was no wonder that Honey Bunch had
supposed them to be from the soda fountain.

"Hello!" said one of the painters, smiling
at the little girl as she stepped out on the
porch.

"Hello!" replied Honey Bunch. "Could I
watch you paint our house?"

The other painter turned around and
laughed. He was short and fat and he had

pleasant blue eyes that twinkled under his
funny, peaked cap.

"I guess we'll have company, Ray," he said
to the painter who had said "Hello" to Honey
Bunch. He was a tall, thin painter and
Honey Bunch thought he looked like the red-
haired boy in the butcher shop.

"Well, we like company," said the painter
called Ray. "Toss me that brush, will you,
Clem?"

So then Honey Bunch knew the fat painter's
name was Clem.

"What's your name?" the fat painter asked,
stirring something in a tin pail.

"My whole name?" asked Honey Bunch
doubtfully, "or the one they call me?"

The fat painter laughed again.

"Why, how many names have you?" he
asked. "You're not such a very big girl,
you know."

"I'm Gertrude Marion Morton," Honey
Bunch told him, "but everybody calls me
Honey Bunch."

"That's the nicest name I ever did hear,"

said the fat painter, stirring away. "We'll
have to paint the house extra nice for a girl
with that name, won't we, Ray?"

Daddy called Honey Bunch just then to
say good-by to her and he told her not to ask
the painters too many questions and to be sure
and not get in their way while they were working. Then he kissed her good-by and went
away to his office where he worked so hard,
Mother said, to buy them pretty dresses to
wear and good food to eat.

Honey Bunch went back to the porch. She
found the painter called Ray trying some
paint on a slab of wood.

"Think you'll like this color for your
house?" he asked her.

Honey Bunch thought it was a very pretty
color. It was yellow, she thought, but the
painter called it "cream." He had other
colors in his paint pots—green and red and
brown and white. He stirred them all with
a stick, one after another, and Honey Bunch
wanted to do it, too.

"Why do you stir it?" she asked, bending

over the pail of green paint and almost putting her small nose into it, so eager was she
to look at the smelly stuff.

The fat painter pulled her back.

"Don't fall in, Sister," he said seriously.
"You wouldn't look pretty with green hair,
would you?   I have to stir the paint to make it
smooth."

"Did you ever see a girl with green hair?"
asked Honey Bunch, sitting down on the steps.

"Well, once," replied the fat painter.
"Once Ray and I worked at a place where
there was a little girl. She was older than
you are.   I think she must have been about
eight or nine. And that girl wouldn't let a
thing alone. One day she climbed up on our
ladder while Ray and I were off at noon hour,
and when she heard us coming back it frightened her so she jumped and her elbow struck a
can of paint—bright green paint it was; it
poured over her as she tumbled down the ladder and I just wish you could have seen that
girl! She had green hair if a child ever had."

Honey Bunch sat quietly, thinking about

the little girl who had upset the paint, while
the men tied the long ropes they had brought
to their ladders and pulled them up to the
top of the house. They began at the top of
the house and painted down, they said.
Honey Bunch, if she had been painting,
would have started at the first floor and gone
up, ending with the roof, because she could
"leave off" on the roof and no one would see
where she had stopped. But then Honey
Bunch had never painted a house. .

Long before the painters had finished their
first day, the little girl tired of watching them.
They worked for hours, standing on the ladder held up by the ropes, painting the cor-
nices and the window frames. Honey Bunch
had thought it would be exciting, but it
wasn't.

The second and the third days they did almost the same things, but the fourth morning
it was much better. They worked at the first
floor, the porches and the porch rails and the
steps. And Honey Bunch could see everything they did and follow them around and

could ask them questions without shouting.

"Can't go up your front steps to-day," said the fat painter to Honey Bunch as soon as he saw her that morning.

"Why can't I?" asked Honey Bunch, smiling. She was pretty sure the fat man was playing a joke on her.

"This says so," the painter answered, holding up a large white card.

It had big black letters on it, but Honey Bunch, although she knew most of her alphabet, could not read words without some one to help her.

"Please, what does it say?" she begged.

"Ray, can you read this?" called the fat painter.

Ray was busily mixing paint, but he turned around and looked at the card.

"It says 'No little girls allowed on these steps,'" he read aloud.

Honey Bunch looked puzzled. She stared at the card.

"How can it say all that?" she said slowly. "There aren't enough letters."

"That's the trouble with Ray," grumbled the fat painter. "He doesn't take time to read properly. I'll tell you what the card says, Sister. It says 'Wet paint.' And you tell your cat that it means she isn't to go walking across the floor I finished last night."

So the painter put the "Wet paint" card up on the steps and he put two pieces of wood across them, too, in case, he said, a person came who couldn't read the card. Then the fat painter and the thin painter went to work and painted every one of the little pieces of wood in the porch railings, on the front porch and the back porch, too.

"It looks so easy," said Honey Bunch to herself. "I just know I could do it. Maybe they would let me, if I asked them."

But the more she thought about it, the surer she was that they wouldn't let her paint.

"I could surprise them," said Honey Bunch, who felt that if she didn't paint something pretty soon she would have to cry. "I wonder if they would like me to paint the back steps?"

Now, although Honey Bunch didn't know it, the back steps were to be left to the very last. The painters were not going to paint them till the front steps were quite dry, for there had to be one dry place for people to walk over to get into the house. Honey Bunch did not know this and she decided to paint the back steps and surprise the painters.

Both men were painting the front cellar window when the little girl trotted around to the back of the house. She knew where to find the pots of paint and the brushes. She thought that the back steps of her house ought to look very nice indeed and what better way to make them look nice than to paint every step a different color? Oh, this was a lovely plan, thought Honey Bunch.

She carefully carried five heavy pails of paint over to the steps and took one of the soft, fat brushes. She had watched the painters long enough to know how they dipped their brushes in and squeezed them against the sides of the pails. Honey Bunch dipped her brush into the yellow paint and began on the top step.

"Just as nice," she said, looking at it when she had been all over the top.

The yellow paint ran down and some got on her shoes, but that did not bother her. She dipped the brush into the green paint and painted the second step.

When she had finished that, there was a great dash of green paint on the front of her pink gingham frock. But even that couldn't bother Honey Bunch.

She painted the third step white and the fourth step red and she was working away, using black paint on the last step when she heard some one come whistling around the corner of the house. It was the Ray painter!

"What *are* you doing?" he asked her, in great surprise.

"I'm painting," answered Honey Bunch, rubbing her hand across her forehead and leaving a smudge of black paint there. "Doesn't it look nice?"

"Well, as long as we have to paint it over.

anyway, I don't see that much harm is done,"
said the Ray painter, looking from the steps
to the little girl and from the little girl back
to the steps. "But I don't think that dress
you have on will ever be the same, Sister."

"I can keep it to paint in," said Honey
Bunch comfortably. "Mother has a dress
she uses to paint in, 'cause it has paint spots
on it, from the time she painted the screens.
Now I have a painting dress, too."

"Well, if you are going into the business,
I'll retire," said the painter, beginning to pick
up the pots of paint and carry them back. "I
never could use as many colors as you do all
at once—it wouldn't be any use for me to try."

CHAPTER XI

THANKSGIVING DINNER

THE painters painted the back steps all one color—a pretty gray—and the next day they took their ropes and ladders and went away. They told Honey Bunch they were going out into the country to paint a farmhouse and three big barns.

Honey Bunch thought the house looked very beautiful. It was cream color and the blinds were green. Mrs. Miller came and washed all the windows, for the paint had spattered on some of them, and she and Mrs. Morton hung up clean, frilly white curtains at the clean windows. Everything looked very nice and cozy and Daddy said he thought they must be ready for winter.

"Well, we are," Honey Bunch's mother told him. "I like to get all the fall work done before it is time to get ready for Thanksgiving."

And of course Honey Bunch wanted to know when it would be Thanksgiving.

"I'll show you," said her daddy, picking her up and carrying her over to the large calendar that hung in the kitchen. "Now this is to-day, Honey Bunch," he said, putting her finger on one of the big blocks. "Count from to-day—one, two, three, four, five, six, seven, eight—Thanksgiving is eight days from to-day."

They had had a fire in the furnace ever since the painters had finished the house. Every morning seemed a little colder. First Honey Bunch put on a warmer dress, then a heavier coat, and at last Mother brought her her mittens. Then Honey Bunch knew it was winter.

"Is eight days a long time, Mother?" asked Honey Bunch when Daddy had gone to the office.

"No, indeed! It is a very short time," answered Mother. "Why, Honey Bunch, you and I have so much to do, we'll have to be as busy as two bees."

Honey Bunch loved to help Mother, and this sounded pleasant.

"What do we have to do, Mother?" she asked eagerly.

"We have to go to market and tell the butcher to save us a good turkey," explained Mother. "We have to make at least three kinds of pies, mince and pumpkin and apple. We have to get Daddy to crack nuts for us and polish red apples. We have to see that our prettiest silver and china is all ready for the table. We have to fix a dinner for the birds—why, Honey Bunch, just think of all the things we have to do and all in eight days!"

"Let's begin right away!" cried Honey Bunch. "Oh, Mother, suppose Thanksgiving came 'fore we were all fixed!"

She and Mother began that very day to get ready for Thanksgiving. They went to market together and Mother told the butcher what kind of turkey she wanted and he promised to send her a nice one the day before Thanksgiving. Then Mother and Honey

Bunch bought nuts and raisins and cranberries
and apples and oranges and a great yellow
pumpkin that Honey Bunch thought was too
pretty to cook. They stopped at the grocery
store and bought eggs and sugar and butter
and so many other good things that the little
girl began to wonder where all the things
were going; she was sure their pantry wouldn't
hold them all.

"Are we thankful Thanksgiving because we
have so much to eat?" she asked her mother,
when they were on their way home.

So Mother told her a little about Thanksgiving, as much as a little girl not yet five
years old could understand; about the Pilgrims who made the first Thanksgiving because they had a good harvest and were very
grateful for food to carry them through the
winter. Honey Bunch asked so many questions about the Pilgrims that they were home
before Mother had answered them all.

"Honey Bunch," said Daddy Morton that
night, "are you going to be too busy to help
me a little?"

"My, no," said the willing little Honey
Bunch, who was always ready to help every
one. "What do you want me to do, Daddy?"

"I'll tell you," answered Daddy. "You
remember the little lame boy I carried the
bouquet to this summer? You picked the
flowers for me, you know, and he was so
pleased he nearly cried. I want to take him a
Thanksgiving basket and I thought perhaps
you would help me pack it."

Honey Bunch was delighted to help, and
the next night Daddy Morton brought home
a pretty round basket with a long handle.
Such fun as he and Honey Bunch had packing
it! They put in little packages of figs,
wrapped in tinfoil paper. They put in dates
and candy, wrapped in goldfoil paper. They
polished apples, and tied a bow of ribbon on
a large bunch of grapes, and tried to make
everything look as pretty as they could.
Wherever there was a little chink left, they
stuffed in raisins and nuts.

"Why are you cracking the nuts, Daddy?"
asked Honey Bunch, when her daddy began

to open several English walnuts carefully with his knife.

"This is a secret, but I'll tell you," he said, smiling. "You watch and see what happens, Honey Bunch."

So Honey Bunch watched, and she saw her daddy take out the nut meats and slip a bright new dime into the shells. Then he glued the two halves together again and really and truly you could not tell those nuts had ever been opened. He did this to a number of nuts and then scattered them around the basket. Honey Bunch stared and stared, but she could not tell which nuts had money in and which had not been opened.

"How will the little boy tell where the money is, Daddy?" she asked anxiously.

"He can't tell," said her daddy. "That is what makes the surprise. He'll crack a nut and it will be good to eat; he'll crack another nut and it will be good to spend. And the basket will amuse him till the last nut is gone."

Honey Bunch thought this was a very nice

plan and she thought about it till bedtime.
Then, when Mother came to kiss her good-
night and put out the light, another thought
popped into her head.

"Mother," she said, "why didn't the Lulu-
man put his card inside a nut shell? Then
it wouldn't get lost and Daddy could have it."

"What made you think of that?" asked
Mother. "I thought you had forgotten the
card long ago. Daddy has, I am quite sure."

But Honey Bunch went to sleep thinking
what a nice little cardcase a nut shell would
make. She dreamed that she went to see the
little lame boy with Daddy and when he
opened the nut shells there was no money in
them, but cunning little cards and every card
said "Lulu."

Honey Bunch and her mother were very
busy till Thanksgiving Day. Mother said she
didn't know what she should do if it wasn't
for Honey Bunch, and Mrs. Miller, who came
the day before Thanksgiving to help, and on
Thanksgiving Day, too, to wash the dishes,

said she knew that Honey Bunch was going
to grow up and be a famous housekeeper.

Just as Honey Bunch had decided that the
calendar was wrong and that Thanksgiving
was still a week away, it came! The pies
Honey Bunch had helped to make were ready,
the table was set with the best tablecloth and
napkins, and the silver was beautifully polished. There were grapes and apples and
oranges all piled into the glass fruit bowl in
the middle of the table. Honey Bunch wore
her best brown velvet dress and Mother wore
her best silk dress and Daddy had on his new
tie. It was Thanksgiving Day and no mistake!

Daddy went off to take the little lame boy
his basket in the morning while Mother and
Honey Bunch stuffed the turkey. Mother
sewed him up with a needle and thread, just as
if he had been a dress she was making.
Honey Bunch said she thought he ought to be
stitched on the sewing machine because Mrs.
Miller had once told her that sewing machine
stitching was very strong indeed; but Mother

said that turkeys were never stitched up on
the machine, so of course it wouldn't do for
their turkey.

When the turkey was in the oven, Mrs.
Miller came and then Honey Bunch and
Mother went into the parlor to watch for
Daddy.

"I shouldn't be surprised if it snowed to-
day," said Mother, pinning back one of the
curtains so they could see out into the street.

"Oh, goody!" cried Honey Bunch, clapping
her hands. "I wish it would snow. I wish
it would snow so much that it would be up
to the roofs of the houses!"

"Why, Honey Bunch, you wouldn't like
that at all," said her mother. "You couldn't
go out for weeks and weeks if that should
happen."

"Why couldn't I?" asked Honey Bunch,
pressing her nose flat against the cold window
pane. "Why couldn't I go out, Mother?"

"Because, if the snow was up to the roofs of
the houses, think how deep it would be," said
Mother. "It would be weeks and weeks be-

fore men could shovel paths through for the trolley cars and the automobiles and for grown-up people to walk. Little children would be buried in snow the moment they put their small feet outdoors."

"Well, then," said Honey Bunch, "I wish it would snow just up to the windows. There comes Daddy!"

She flew to the door to meet him and to ask him if the little lame boy liked his basket.

"Don't tell me I smell turkey!" cried Daddy Morton, wrinkling his nose. "Honey Bunch, do you know whether we are going to have turkey for dinner to-day?"

Honey Bunch giggled and nodded.

"Yes, we are," she answered. "I helped Mother fix it, Daddy. He is all sewed up with a needle and thread. Did the little lame boy like his basket?"

"To be sure he did," said Daddy Morton. "I left him eating grapes and looking at the rest of the things when I came away. And if you'll look inside this parcel, Edith," he added, handing a long package to Honey

Bunch's mother, "you'll find something for yourself."

Honey Bunch came close to Mother to watch her open the parcel. Inside were great, beautiful yellow chrysanthemums, raggedy, handsome flowers whose smell reminded Honey Bunch of the woods where she had gone one Saturday afternoon with Daddy.

"Oh, David, how lovely!" cried Mrs. Morton. "We'll have them on the table. Honey Bunch, aren't they beautiful?"

Honey Bunch spent the morning trotting back and forth between the parlor and the kitchen. She saw Mrs. Miller "baste" the turkey, which had nothing to do with needle and thread. Honey Bunch had seen Mother baste her dresses, often, but when Mrs. Miller basted the turkey, she poured spoonfuls of gravy over it. Honey Bunch helped Mother fill the little candy and salted nut dishes and tasted a candy and a nut or two. She tied an orange ribbon on Lady Clare. And then, finally, dinner was ready.

Every year Mrs. Morton invited three old

ladies who lived in an old ladies' home to
come to Thanksgiving dinner. They were
sisters and their names were Miss Anna, Miss
Mary and Miss Bertha Anderson. Mother
told Honey Bunch that they were not exactly
poor and they were not hungry; they were
well taken care of in the home.

"But they are lonely, for they have no one of
their own to love them," she said. "No nice
daddy, no little girl. I like them to come
and be happy with us, and Daddy does, too."

Honey Bunch did not talk very much dur-
ing dinner. Miss Mary talked a great deal
and Miss Anna and Miss Bertha talked, too.
They seemed to be hungry and they liked the
dinner. Honey Bunch was sure they did. It
was a very good dinner and Daddy gave
Honey Bunch the wishbone of the turkey.
She put it away to dry and then she intended
to make a wish with it.

CHAPTER XII

THE FIRST SNOW

WHEN dinner was over, Honey Bunch whispered to her mother that she would like to go outdoors and play a little while. The three old ladies wanted to sit in the parlor and knit and talk and that, of course, wasn't very exciting for a little girl.

"Don't go far away from the house," said Mother, kissing Honey Bunch and coming out into the hall to help her into her coat. "And if you are cold, come in right away."

Honey Bunch jumped off the steps, two steps at a time. It was cold and there was no sunshine. The gray clouds seemed pretty close to the ground. Honey Bunch thought that she could have touched one, if she had been just a little taller.

"Oh-hoo, Honey Bunch!" called Ida Camp, waving to her and hurrying across the street.

"We had my aunt from the country for dinner!"

"We had three old ladies," said Honey Bunch.

"Oh, dear, it's raining!" cried Ida, as something wet struck her in the eyes. "I think it's mean to rain."

"It's snow!" cried Honey Bunch. "Ida, it's snowing!"

"It's snowing! It's snowing!" children began to shriek up and down the street. "It's snowing! It's snowing!" they cried, dancing up and down in delight.

You would have thought, from the noise they made, that they had never seen snow before.

"Hurrah! We're going to have a blizzard!" shouted Elmer Gray, a little boy who lived two or three doors from Honey Bunch. "It's going to be a blizzard and maybe there won't be any school the rest of the winter," he cried.

"That Elmer Gray makes a lot of fuss about everything," said Ida. "Come on over to my

house, Honey Bunch, and let's make ice-
cream."

"I told Mother I wouldn't go away from
our house," replied Honey Bunch. "Can't we
make ice-cream here?"

"I don't remember how you make it, without asking," said Ida, "but we can ask your
mother."

They went in and found Mrs. Miller just
putting away the last clean dish in the kitchen.

"Don't be bothering your mother, Honey
Bunch," she said, when she heard what the
two little girls wanted. "I'll tell you all about
snow ice-cream. You take clean snow, a
saucerful, and a little sugar and some vanilla
and stir it up. And if you eat too much of
it you'll be sick sure."

"We'll not eat too much of it, shall we,
Ida?" said Honey Bunch. "Will you give us
the sugar, Mrs. Miller?"

"If you can find enough ice-cream, bring
it in and I'll help you," said good-natured
Mrs. Miller. "I don't believe you can find
enough snow."

But the flakes were whirling now and the
ground was already white. There was not
enough snow to scrape up, that is, clean snow,
but Mrs. Miller said she had to do several
more things before it was time for her to go
home and she thought they could scrape up
two saucerfuls of snow before she went. Sure
enough, in another half hour, the snow was
deep enough to sweep off the steps and Honey
Bunch and Ida carefully took off some clean
snow from the kitchen window sills.

"Now I'll pour in a drop of vanilla, like
this," said Mrs. Miller, holding the vanilla
bottle first over one saucer and then the other.
"And then in goes the powdered sugar, like
this——" and she carefully put in the powdered sugar. "Now then, Honey Bunch and
Ida, stir away, and don't make yourselves
sick."

Honey Bunch and Ida carried their saucers
out into the yard to eat the ice-cream. It tasted
very good, and it was, as Honey Bunch said,
"as cold as real ice-cream."

"I have to go home now," Ida said, when she had finished her saucer. "My aunt is going away on the train and I have to say good-by to her."

After Ida had gone, Honey Bunch made herself a little slide on the walk in front of the house. She was having a very good time, sliding up and down and singing a little song to herself, when some one came sliding in back of her and bumped into her so hard she nearly lost her balance and fell. It was Elmer Gray.

"Who made the slide?" he asked.

"I did," said Honey Bunch. "Want to slide?"

"It isn't much of a slide," replied Elmer. "You ought to see the one I had last year outside the school yard. It was a dandy, only the janitor put ashes on it, because so many people fell on it."

"I like my own slide," said Honey Bunch happily. "Aren't you glad it is snowing, Elmer?"

"Sure I am. I have a new sled," answered
Elmer. "Had your face washed yet, Honey
Bunch?"

Honey Bunch looked at Elmer a little
doubtfully. He could be very nice. Once he
had climbed a tree and brought Lady Clare
down for her when the cat was afraid to come
down herself. But Elmer could also tease.
Honey Bunch remembered once when he had
frightened her very much by showing her a
live mouse.

"Have to have your face washed the first
time it snows," said Elmer, scooping up a
handful of snow. "Gives you nice red cheeks.
Come on, Honey Bunch, let me wash your
face for you."

He came running toward her and Honey
Bunch turned and ran. She ran as hard as
she could, up the street, and Elmer chased
her, calling at every step:

"Let me wash your face, Honey Bunch!
Let me wash your face for you!"

Honey Bunch was very sure she did not
want her face washed with snow, but Elmer

could run much faster than she could and he
would surely have caught her if he had not
dropped his handful of snow and stopped to
scoop up another. Honey Bunch, running,
dodged around some one on the walk, but
Elmer ran right into the tall figure as he
scrambled to his feet with the snow in his
hand.

"Here! Where are you bound for?" asked
the some one.

"It's Ned!" cried Honey Bunch.

Ned Camp was Ida's oldest brother. He
was in high school and Honey Bunch thought
he must be quite grown up. Almost as old
as Daddy Morton, perhaps.

"Honey Bunch, is Elmer teasing you?"
asked Ned, holding Elmer by his coat sleeve.

"I wasn't!" said Elmer.

"No, I guess he isn't teasing me," replied
Honey Bunch slowly, for she was out of
breath from running.

"You thought you'd wash her face with
snow, didn't you?" said Ned, surprising both

Elmer and Honey Bunch, who did not see how he could ever have guessed the truth. "Well, Honey Bunch, I'll hold this young man for you while you wash his face, if you like."

Honey Bunch shook her head.

"I don't want to," she said.

"Then I'll do it for you," promised Ned, and he grabbed up a handful of snow and, in spite of Elmer's kicking and wriggling, he rubbed his face thoroughly with the cold, wet flakes.

"This will do you good," said Ned, rolling Elmer in the snow when he had finished and then standing him upright again and brushing him off. "Now if you want to fight me, Son, go to it!"

But Elmer, who was really a good-tempered lad, if he did like to torment his friends now and then, only laughed.

"I don't care, Ned Camp!" he cried. "You wait till you want some one to pick up balls for you next spring!"

Ned played baseball on the high school

team and Elmer often went to watch them
play and brought back the balls when they
went out of bounds.

"Don't threaten me!" said Ned, pretending
to be angry and starting for Elmer, who ran
off home as fast as he could go, Ned chasing
him through the snow.

Honey Bunch ran after them, for she remembered that she was not supposed to go
away from the house. She found her daddy
out on the steps looking for her and when she
told him about Elmer, he understood that she
could not help running off.

Not very long after Thanksgiving, early
in December, a most important day came.
The day was Honey Bunch's birthday. This
year she would be five years old.

"Will I have five candles on my birthday
cake, Mother?" she asked, a week or so before her birthday.

"Yes, indeed, dear," answered Mrs. Morton. "Five candles and that means five birthday wishes."

"And that isn't all," said Daddy Morton who was reading his paper on the other side of the table. "There will be——"

"David! Sh!" cried Mrs. Morton, holding up her finger.

"Is it a secret?" asked Honey Bunch. "Oh, Mother, is it a secret? Is it about my birthday, Mother?"

"Yes, it is a secret," her mother admitted, laughing. "You and your daddy are just alike, Honey Bunch; you are both bound to let the cat out of the bag. But this is one secret you will not be able to guess before the time comes. I am going to surprise you and you'll never guess what the surprise is."

And though Honey Bunch wondered and wondered, when her birthday came she had not been able to guess the secret.

CHAPTER XIII

BIRTHDAY SURPRISES

"When did Daddy put Lady Clare in the rag bag?" asked Honey Bunch thoughtfully, tasting her good oatmeal.

It was the morning of her birthday and she was five years old. Mother and Daddy had each kissed her five times before breakfast and here she was at the table eating oatmeal from a brand new blue bowl that, Mother said, was a present from Mrs. Miller.

"I put Lady Clare in the rag bag? Never!" said Daddy Morton, looking puzzled. "Is the cat lost, Honey Bunch?"

Honey Bunch shook her head.

"No-o, Lady Clare isn't lost," she answered. "But—but Mother said you let the cat out of the bag. Didn't you, Mother?"

"I said he usually did and sometimes you helped," said Mrs. Morton, laughing. "Only,

Honey Bunch, Mother wasn't speaking of rag
bags; I meant that you and Daddy like to tell
secrets before the right time."

Honey Bunch didn't see what secrets had to
do with cats in bags, but she wisely decided
not to think about that any longer. It was
much more exciting to think about her birthday and the surprises that were going to happen. Mother had said there would be surprises.

"Now, Honey Bunch," said Mother when
breakfast was over, "Daddy and I decided
that you would have a better time if you
didn't have your presents all at once. They
are hidden around the house and I think
you'll find them without much trouble. And
this noon Ida's mother has asked you to have
lunch with them."

Honey Bunch kissed Daddy good-by, her
mind filled with thoughts of presents in tissue paper. Then, too, it would be fun to go
to Ida's house for lunch. Last year Ida had
come to Honey Bunch's house on her birth-

day and they had had a party supper together.

"Now I'm five years old, I'm big enough to go visiting, I guess," said Honey Bunch to herself.

"Honey Bunch," called Mrs. Morton from the kitchen, "will you run upstairs and get me a clean handkerchief? You know where I keep them—in that little box in my top drawer."

Honey Bunch ran upstairs and into her mother's room. She found the handkerchief box in the top drawer of the bureau, but there was something in the box besides handkerchiefs. The something was a little white package, tied with pink ribbon and with a little card tied to the ribbon.

"Oh—my!" said Honey Bunch softly. "That's a birthday present! I just know it's a birthday present!"

She did not forget to take a handkerchief for Mother, but how fast she ran downstairs! She burst into the kitchen waving the little white box.

"Mother!" she cried. "Mother! Look!
Is it a birthday present? And it's for me,
isn't it, Mother?"

Mrs. Morton looked at the card on the box.
"Why, dear, this is printed and you can
read it," she said. "See, Daddy has made the
letters very plain: 'To Honey Bunch with
dear love from her daddy.' What do you suppose is inside?"

Honey Bunch sat down on the floor to open
the package. Inside the white tissue paper
she found a little white box. And inside the
box, on a nest of pink cotton, was a small gold
locket and chain.

"Oh, Mother!" Honey Bunch held up the
locket for her mother to see. "Look what
Daddy gave me! I can wear it to Ida's
house, can't I, Mother?"

Mother said she might wear the locket and
chain and then she offered to fasten the clasp
around Honey Bunch's neck and, turning the
locket over, the little girl found that her ini-
tials were engraved on one side of the locket—
G. M. M.—and on the other side was a little

flower, a blue flower that her mother said was
a forget-me-not.

Honey Bunch was very proud of her new
locket, and when the postman rang the doorbell, she danced to the door to show it to him.

"Well, well, that *is* a pretty locket," said
the postman. "You don't mean to tell me you
have a birthday to-day? How old are you?"

"I'm five years old," said Honey Bunch.
"And I'm going to have five candles on my
birthday cake."

"I didn't know you were five years old, but
if you are, I think I have a parcel for you,"
said the postman. "It's for a girl who is five
years old to-day and as you're the first little
girl I've seen who has a birthday this morning, I think I'll give this to you," and the jolly
postman held out a flat brown package to
Honey Bunch.

"Mother!" shouted Honey Bunch, tumbling
upstairs, for she knew her mother was making the beds now. "Mother! The postman
brought me something because I'm five years
old!"

"Well, you are having an exciting morning," said Mrs. Morton. "Let me cut the string for you, dear. There—you dropped the card, Honey Bunch. That will tell you who sent the present. Why, it is from Miss Anna and Miss Bertha and Miss Mary!"

They were the three old ladies, you remember, who lived in the Old Ladies' Home and who came to Honey Bunch's house for Thanksgiving dinner. Miss Anna had knit the little girl a pretty blue sweater. Miss Bertha had made a smaller sweater for her doll. Miss Mary had knitted a round cap for the doll.

"Aren't they lovely, Honey Bunch, to do all that work for you?" said Honey Bunch's mother. "It takes a good many hours to make a sweater, and those dear old ladies must have knitted pretty steadily to finish this gift in time for your birthday. I remember they asked me Thanksgiving Day when you would be five years old."

Honey Bunch liked her sweater very much indeed and she said she would wear it to Ida's house and also take Eleanor, in her new sweater and cap, with her to show Ida.

"That will be all right, won't it, Mother?" asked Honey Bunch. "Because this is my birthday."

And Mother kissed her and said that people could do almost as they pleased on their birthdays and she thought it would be very nice for Honey Bunch and Eleanor to wear their new sweaters.

"I wonder if you'll have time to dust the hall table for me, Honey Bunch?" said Mother. "I'd like the house to look tidy on your birthday. Be sure you dust the lower shelf, dearie."

Honey Bunch loved to be useful, and she trotted downstairs and took the silk duster out of the bag in the back hall where it was always kept. Then she dusted off the top of the hall table very carefully and put the velvet runner exactly in the center.

Some little girls I know do not dust the lower shelves of the tables in their houses. They think that no one can see the dust there. But Honey Bunch was not like that. She began to dust the lower shelf of the hall table quite as carefully as she had dusted the top.

Away back, in the corner of the shelf, near the wall, her dust cloth hit something hard. It was a box!

Honey Bunch reached under and pulled out the box. Dear me, it was another birthday present!

Honey Bunch threw the duster down and started for the stairs. Her mother was just coming down.

"Mother!" cried Honey Bunch. "Look! Another present!"

She and Mother sat down on the stairs and opened the box right away. Inside there was a slip of paper that read "To my Honey Bunch with love from Mother."

Honey Bunch had to stop then and kiss Mother and then she went on to open the box.

Inside was a trunk, a doll's trunk, and inside the trunk was a small doll and "enough clothes to last her a year," as Daddy said when he saw them that night. Honey Bunch had wanted a "little doll" for a long time, and

she was so pleased with this gift that she
hugged Mother again and named the doll
"Edith" right on the spot. She already had
three dolls named for her mother but, as she
explained, she could change their names eas-
ily.

Before it was time for Honey Bunch to go
to Ida's she had found three more gifts; a
set of dolls' furniture in the box where her best
shoes were kept; new hair-ribbons in her own
handkerchief box; and a glass jar of candy
standing on the shelf where the toothpaste
was in the bathroom.

"Daddy did that," said Mrs. Morton, when
Honey Bunch called her to come and see.
"He said he thought if you found some candy
on that shelf you might remember more eas-
ily to brush your teeth."

When Honey Bunch was dressed in her
pretty blue and white challis dress, with Miss
Anna's sweater over it and her locket and
chain around her neck, she looked just like
a birthday girl. Her mother said so.

"I'd like to take Edith, but she's so small

she couldn't sit at the table," said Honey
Bunch. "And then Eleanor knows Mrs.
Camp and Edith doesn't."

So the Eleanor doll in her new sweater and
cap went to Ida's house for lunch with her
little mother and the new doll stayed at
home.

Ida was very glad to see Honey Bunch.
So was Mrs. Camp. There were only the
two little girls and Ida's mother at the lunch-
eon table, for Ned did not come home from
school at noon. Eleanor had a seat next to
Honey Bunch, and though she did not say a
word she smiled all the time, and no one can
find fault with a doll who always smiles.

Mrs. Camp said that as it was Honey
Bunch's birthday, she thought she would have
pink roses for the center of her table, and
very beautiful the flowers looked. Honey
Bunch thought they did not look exactly like
the pink roses she remembered in her garden
in summer, but she was too polite to ask questions.

"We have creamed chicken, 'cause this is

your birthday," said Ida, when they sat down
at the table.

They had little baskets of candy, chocolate
drops in spun sugar baskets, at each place and
a pretty paper doll with "Honey Bunch" and
"Ida" written in gold letters on the skirts.
And from each place a pink ribbon streamer
ran back to the bunch of roses.

"When will it be time for me to give Honey
Bunch her present, Mother?" Ida asked, when
the maid had brought in the vanilla ice-cream
and the round, pink-iced cakes that went
with it.

"I think you might give it to her now,"
said Mrs. Camp.

So Ida slipped off her chair and went into
the parlor and came back in a moment with
a bundle which she gave to Honey Bunch, a
little shyly.

"I wish you many happy returns of the
day," she said politely.

Honey Bunch let her ice-cream melt while
she opened the bundle. In it was a rag dog,
a rag cat and two rag puppies and two rag

kittens. They were stuffed with soft cotton
and painted and they looked very real indeed.

"Lady Clare won't mind that kind, will
she?" said Ida.

Honey Bunch was so happy she could
hardly talk. Ida had a set of rag animals
like this and she had played with them often.
She had wished she could have rag dogs of
her own, and now here they were, and exactly
the kind Ida had.

"I love you very much, Ida," said Honey
Bunch. And there is no better way to say
"thank you" for a birthday gift, or any other
kind of gift, is there?

"Don't forget to pull your ribbons," said
Mrs. Camp, smiling at the two little friends.

Then Honey Bunch learned she was supposed to pull the pink ribbon at her place.
The bouquet of roses fell apart—they were
make-believe flowers—and tied to the other
end of the ribbons were little favors. Honey
Bunch had a set of celluloid animals that
would float and Ida had a soap bubble set.

"And now let's play," suggested Ida, as

though she had been anxious to play with
Honey Bunch for several minutes.

They were having a grand time with the
soap bubble set and the rag animals, to say
nothing of floating the celluloid ducks in the
bathtub, when Mrs. Camp came upstairs and
said it was time for Honey Bunch to go home.

"I hate to break up your fun, dear," she
said, "but I promised your mother you would
be home at three o'clock. And it is five minutes of, now."

"Oh, Mother!" cried Ida, "we're just beginning to have a good time. Couldn't you telephone Mrs. Morton that Honey Bunch will
be home at four o'clock?"

"I couldn't," said Mrs. Camp, shaking her
head. "I promised this little girl should be
at home at three o'clock, and home she must
be when the clock strikes three."

So Honey Bunch took off the oilcloth apron
Mrs. Camp had tied over her frock to keep
it dry, and she put the ducks back in the box
and wrapped up the rag animals and took
her candy basket in one hand and shook hands

with Mrs. Camp with the other. Then she
picked up Eleanor and started downstairs.

"I've had a lovely time," said Honey
Bunch.

Then she kissed Ida and trotted across the
street to her own house. The clock on the
mantel struck three just as Honey Bunch
stepped up on the porch. Some one inside
opened the door for her.

CHAPTER XIV

FIVE COUSINS

HONEY BUNCH tried to look behind the door. She thought perhaps her daddy had come home and was hiding from her. But it was not Daddy Morton back of the front door.

"Boo!" cried some one, and her cousin, Bobby Turner, jumped out at her.

"Hello!" he said, laughing at Honey Bunch who was so surprised she couldn't think of a word to say.

"Hello!" "Hello!" "Hello!" three little voices cried, and three little girls came running out of the parlor.

They were cousins, too, Tess, Bobby's twin sister, Julie Somerset, and Mary Morton who was always called "Stub." Her nickname had been given her because she was a little girl who stubbed her toes very often when she

walked. She never minded it, either being
called "Stub" or stubbing her toes, and she
was so good-natured that she made "Stub"
seem a jolly kind of name for a girl to have.

"Are you surprised?" asked Stub, giving
Honey Bunch a kiss.

"Of course I'm s'prised," said Honey
Bunch. "Isn't it nice? Does Mother know
you've come?"

"She invited us," laughed Bobby. "We all
came on the two-thirty train. Say, Honey
Bunch, we thought you were never coming
home."

The cousins were the surprise Mother and
Daddy had planned for Honey Bunch on her
birthday. Daddy had almost told her, but
Mother had stopped him in time.

"That's why Mother told Mrs. Camp I
must come home at three o'clock," thought
Honey Bunch, following the cousins back into
the parlor where her mother was.

Truth to tell, Honey Bunch felt the least
bit shy with these four cousins. They did not

live near and she saw them only "once in a while," as Bobby said. Stub was nearest her age, and Stub was six years old. She lived, Honey Bunch knew, on a large farm in the country, a farm where Honey Bunch's father had often gone when he was a little boy.

Julie Somerset was a little brown girl, about seven years old. She had blue eyes, but her skin was brown because she played on the beach so much. Julie lived at the seashore and she could tell you all about shells and little sand crabs and when she grew up she meant to have a sailboat of her own and go fishing every day.

The twins were the oldest of the cousins. They were eight, going on nine, and they, of course, went to school and knew a great deal about arithmetic and geography. They knew about other things, too, for they lived in New York City and crossed two car tracks to go to school every morning. Bobby took care of Tess, who was careless, and when he wasn't laughing at her he was helping her with her lessons or mending something for her. Tess broke the toys and Bobby mended them and that was surely a very good plan.

"What's in the bundle?" asked Stub, pointing to the package Honey Bunch carried.

"Those are my rag animals," explained the birthday girl, unwrapping the parcel. "Ida Camp gave them to me."

She showed them the things she had brought home from Ida's and her locket and chain and the other gifts she had found around the house that morning. Before she had finished showing and explaining, all five cousins were chattering away as though they had always lived in the same house.

"Did you have any snow Thanksgiving?" asked Stub. "We went coasting in the afternoon and I steered right into a tree."

"Gee, we had only a few flakes in New York," said Bobby. "Anyway, when it does snow, they shovel it off the streets so fast we can't have any fun. I'd like to see a real snowstorm just once and build a fort."

Julie said it had rained at the seashore over

the holiday, and she added that she didn't like snow.

"I like to play in it," said Honey Bunch. "I wished it would snow up to the roof of the houses on Thanksgiving, but Mother said the trolley cars couldn't run if it was as deep as that."

"The deepest snow there ever was wouldn't bother New York," boasted Bobby.

But before the others could ask him what he meant, Daddy Morton came in and Mother with him.

"Let's have a fire so we can see how these cousins really look," said Daddy Morton, smiling. "I like to see faces in the glow of a wood fire. How about it, Bobby?"

"I'll help you build a fire, Uncle David," cried Bobby eagerly, and he went down cellar with his uncle and helped him bring up some wood and the kindling to start the fire.

"I'll sit down a little while and enjoy the fire before I begin to get supper," said Mrs. Morton, dropping down on the divan and taking Honey Bunch in her lap. Stub sat on one side of her and Julie on the other and Tess and Bobby sat on either arm of Daddy Morton's big arm chair.

"Now that's what I call a good blaze!" said Daddy Morton, as the flames roared up the chimney. "Stub knows what a wood fire is, don't you, Stubbie?"

Stub smiled and nodded.

"When it snows, or is very cold, Daddy keeps the fireplace going all night," she said. "He puts in a big back log and it will smolder all night and start a fire in the morning."

"Oh, Bobby!" Honey Bunch sat up straight so suddenly she almost bumped Mother's chin. "Bobby, you said the biggest snow there ever was wouldn't bother New York. Why wouldn't it?"

"Bobby, are you boasting about New York already?" asked Daddy Morton, laughing at Bobby, who turned a little red but looked determined.

"Well, Honey Bunch said if the snow came up to the roofs here the trolley cars wouldn't run," he said.

"Can the trolley cars run when the snow is up to the roofs in New York?" asked Stub. "I don't believe it."

"I didn't say they could," said Bobby. "I never saw snow up to the roof. But if it did snow and snow and snow, you could still ride on the subways; snow wouldn't stop them."

Honey Bunch was so excited her hair-ribbon stood straight up. Her cheeks were as red as the heart of the fire.

"Subways!" she cried in amazement. "Oh, Bobby, how can you ride on him?"

Tess laughed and Bobby stared at his little cousin.

"Him?" he repeated. "Who said anything about *him?* What are you talking about, Honey Bunch? I said *subways,* not *him.*"

"But that's a him," persisted Honey Bunch. "He's a man. You can't ride on a man, Bobby Turner. I don't believe you can, even in New York."

Daddy and Mother Morton looked at each other smiling. The other children looked at Honey Bunch. Every one thought the little girl did not understand what Bobby was saying.

"Now you listen, Honey Bunch Morton," said Bobby slowly, the way he spoke when he was explaining an arithmetic lesson to his sister, Tess. "The subway is a railroad; they run all about New York, deep down in the ground. No matter how much it snows or rains up in the streets, none of it gets into the subways. They're always warm and dry. When you come to see us, Mother will take us all riding on them, won't she, Tess?"

"I guess I know!" cried Honey Bunch, very much in earnest. "Mr. Subways was a *man*. He isn't any old railroad under the ground. He came to see Daddy and Daddy wasn't home—he'd gone to Washington. So there!"

This time it was Mrs. Morton who sat up very straight. Her cheeks were almost as red as those of Honey Bunch.

"David! That was the name of the man who came to see you!" she said eagerly. "Mr.

Subways—of course! I remember it now!
And it was such an odd name I thought I'd
be sure to remember it always!"

"He was a man, wasn't he, Mother?" said
Honey Bunch.

"I should say he was!" answered Daddy
Morton, looking pleased. "I know who he is
perfectly well. I'll send him a night letter
after supper. That case has taken a turn
again to-day, Edith," he added to Honey
Bunch's mother, "and I think Mr. Subways
and I can probably save several thousand dol-
lars."

Honey Bunch was so glad she had remembered the name of the man that she was willing to let Bobby insist that subways were
really a system of railroads that ran underground. Honey Bunch did not really think
a railroad could run underground, and Julie
and Stub were inclined to agree with her.
But Tess and Bobby said that every one rode
on the subways in New York.

"Wait till you come to see us and we'll show
you," promised Bobby.

"Maybe I won't want to ride under the ground," said Honey Bunch.

But she did—oh, my, yes, she did, of course —when she went to the big city of New York to visit Bobby and Tess. When she went visiting and what happened to her in that great city I'll tell you by and by.

Mrs. Morton had gone out to get supper ready while the children talked, and in a few minutes she came back to ask them to come out into the dining-room.

"Oh—ah!" every one cried, and no wonder. In the middle of the table was a beautiful white birthday cake with five pink candles blazing merrily. *"Honey Bunch—5 years old"* was written on the top of the cake in chocolate icing. There was a red "cracker" at each child's plate and two platters of sand-wiches and a cup of cocoa for each one with whipped cream floating on the top.

"Make your wishes, Honey Bunch," said her daddy, lifting her up to stand on her chair. "Make your wishes and blow out the candles."

Honey Bunch shut her eyes very tight and

made four wishes. She couldn't think of another, so she opened her eyes and blew. Four candles sputtered and died out and Daddy blew on the fifth and that stopped burning.

"Only four of your wishes will come true," said Bobby, as they sat down.

"I made only four," answered Honey Bunch. "One was that it would snow and one was that Lady Clare could sleep on my bed and one was that I could have all the candy I want and the other was Daddy would stay home and play with me all day."

They all laughed, and Daddy Morton said that she wouldn't need him now she had four cousins to play with.

"They'll be here all day to-morrow, Honey Bunch," he said, "and you must play every game you can think of. You don't often have four playfellows, do you?"

"Let's play hide-and-seek," suggested Stub. "This would be a dandy house for a game like that."

"How do you know?" asked Bobby. "You never saw this house before."

"Yes, I have," said Stub. "Haven't I been here before, Aunt Edith? Once when I was six months old, Mother brought me. She told me so."

"I don't believe you can remember much about the house," grumbled Bobby, but it was decided that the next day the five cousins should have a grand game of hide-and-seek.

"Make as much noise as you want," said Honey Bunch's mother. "I don't mind noise at all."

CHAPTER XV

HIDE-AND-SEEK

THE next morning Stub announced that they must have all the fun they could because she had to go home that afternoon. Tess and Bobby and Julie were going home, too. They all attended school, and when you go to school it is very important not to miss a single day. Stub said it was lucky Honey Bunch had her birthday on Friday, because she had to miss only the part of school that "didn't count."

"Fridays, in the morning we go walking for flowers and plants and things," explained Stub. "And afternoons we recite; so it doesn't matter if you do miss Friday at school."

"How can you look for plants when it's winter?" asked Tess, who was a city girl. "Nothing grows in the winter time."

"Some things do," said Stub. "And our

teacher makes us tell the different kinds of trees from the bark. I guess you can't tell a maple tree when it hasn't any leaves on, just by looking at the bark, can you?"

"I don't know a maple tree, anyway," replied Tess. "But I know all about the pictures in the Art Museum. I'll bet you don't."

They might have gone on talking about their schools all the morning if Bobby, who didn't see any sense in talking of school when there was something else to do, had not suggested that they play some game.

"I thought we were going to play hide-and-seek," he said. "Aunt Edith said we could make all the noise we wanted to."

Bobby liked to make a noise. Sometimes his daddy said he could make more noise than any boy on the block.

"All right, let's play hide-and-seek," agreed Honey Bunch. She loved to hear the children talk about school, but she was an unselfish little girl and always tried to do as she thought her friends wanted her to. If Bobby wanted to play, she was willing.

The little girls would have liked to play with the dolls, but of course dolls didn't interest Bobby. He had suggested, at breakfast, that Honey Bunch let him see if he could hit the birds who came to the yard to eat the bread Mother threw out for them with the rag animals Ida had given Honey Bunch.

"They're so soft they won't hurt a bird," argued Bobby. "I'd like to see if I could hit a sparrow at long range."

But Honey Bunch wouldn't hear of this, so there was nothing left for Bobby to do but play games.

"I'll be 'It' the first time," said Tess good-naturedly. "We'll go upstairs, and it's no fair hiding anywhere off the second floor. Hurry up."

The five children ran upstairs, Honey Bunch with cheeks as pink as roses. She had not known what fun it was to have four cousins to play with. She was used to amusing herself, and this having company, she thought, was about the nicest thing that had ever happened to her.

Upstairs, Tess hid her face in the soft pillow on Mrs. Morton's bed and the other children tiptoed away to hide. Bobby crawled under a couch, Stub climbed into the clothes hamper in the hall, Julie hid behind a chair in the sewing room, and Honey Bunch wrapped herself in the curtain that hung between her own room and her daddy's and mother's room.

"One-two-three-four-five——" began Tess, counting aloud. She counted up to ten. Then she opened her eyes and started to look for the others.

While she was exploring the hall Julie and Bobbie ran "home" safe, and when she was poking the couch pillows in the guest room Stub climbed out of the hamper and ran into Mrs. Morton's room without being seen. But Honey Bunch, who didn't know how to play as well as the others, waited till she heard Tess walking past her and then jumped out and said "Boo!"

Tess had to laugh, and the others laughed, too, and Honey Bunch laughed with them, though she didn't know what they were laughing about.

"Now you have to be 'It,'" said Tess to her little cousin. "You mustn't let the one who is 'It' see you before you get home, Honey Bunch. Come on, we'll hide. Honey Bunch is 'It.'"

"She didn't understand, so I don't think it's fair to make her be 'It,'" said Bobby sturdily. "You give her another chance, Tess."

"I'd like to be 'It,'" cried Honey Bunch. "I'd like it just as much! You go hide."

So Honey Bunch buried her head in the pillow on her mother's bed and counted as she had heard Tess do. Every one got home safe except Bobby. He really let Honey Bunch find him, because he didn't want her to have to be "It" again.

"Hide all over the house," said Bobby generously. "I don't care where you hide. I'll find you or tag you before you get in. And I'll count twenty-five, too, so you'll have all the time you want to hide."

This was most exciting, and the children scattered as Bobby began to count.

"Let's hide together—you and me," whispered Tess to Honey Bunch. "Where is a good place? Some place Bobby will never think to look."

"In the back hall there's a closet where Mother keeps the brooms and dust cloths," said Honey Bunch.

"All right, we'll hide there—come on," answered Tess, pulling Honey Bunch along by the hand.

They reached the closet. It was large and deep. There were brooms and dust cloths and a dust pan hanging in neat little racks against the wall and several pails and mops. Mrs. Miller did not like to have to go down to the kitchen to get a pail when she wanted to wipe up the second-story floors.

"This is a good place," said Tess, pulling the door close after them. "I don't believe Bobby will ever look here."

The back hall was a little shut off from the rest of the house by an archway and you did

not see the closet door at all when you looked
through the arch.

"There, he's begun to hunt," said Tess,
peeping through the small crack she had left.
"Oh, my, he's coming this way!"

She pulled the door shut. There was a little click. It was perfectly dark in the closet
and rather warm.

"Where is he now?" whispered Honey
Bunch, holding fast to Tess's hand.

"Sh!" whispered back Tess. "He's out in
the other hall. I hear him opening and shut-
ting doors."

The two little girls sat very still for what
seemed a long time to Honey Bunch. Once
or twice they thought they heard laughter,
as though Bobby had found the hiding
place of some one. Then it was quite still
again.

"Do you know what I think?" said Tess,
"I think he's sitting out there in the hall, near
the stairs. Then he can see every one who
tries to come up or down. Well, he won't
catch us that way."

"No, he won't catch us that way," repeated Honey Bunch.

By and by Tess said she thought they might venture out.

"We can go down the back stairs and up the other way," she said. "Even if we're tagged, I'd rather be 'It' than stay in this hot closet any longer."

"Yes, let's go," said Honey Bunch.

Tess fumbled with the door a few minutes.

"Why, Honey Bunch, where's the knob on this door?" she asked in surprise.

"It's there," answered Honey Bunch. "I'll open it for you."

But though Honey Bunch passed her little hands all over the place where the door knob ought to be, she couldn't find it.

"Hasn't it any door knob?" asked Tess crossly. "All our doors at home have door knobs."

"Course we have door knobs," said Honey Bunch. "I'll find it in a minute."

But the more she tried to find it, the more it seemed that she must have made a mistake.

"I'm so hot that I don't know what to do," declared Tess. "Suppose we never get out of here, Honey Bunch? I don't believe we ever shall!"

Honey Bunch felt like crying. She was hot, too, and she certainly didn't want to stay in that dark closet all the rest of her life.

"I'll kick on the door," she said hopefully. "Mother will come and get us."

But though she kicked and Tess helped her kick, no one came.

"Doesn't any one ever come to this closet?" asked Tess.

"Mrs. Miller does," replied Honey Bunch. "She comes Fridays to clean and she uses the mops that are in here."

"Then we'll have to stay here till Friday," said Tess, who was not feeling very cheerful that morning. "To-day is Saturday. We'll have to stay in here a week and my mother won't know where I am and your mother won't know where you are."

Two tears rolled down Honey Bunch's cheeks.

"I'll kick some more," she said bravely. "We could kick it down, maybe."

"I think we'd better yell," said Tess. "Your mother might not like us to kick the door down."

So both together, they shouted. In a few moments they heard Bobby shouting, too, and he was screaming: "Where are you? Where are you?"

"In the closet!" cried Tess and Honey Bunch. "In the hall closet!"

Then Bobby and Julie and Stub came running into the back hall and the girls in the closet heard them fumbling at the door. It opened and the rush of light made Honey Bunch blink her eyes.

"Why didn't you open the door?" asked Bobby. "We waited and waited for you and then I heard you making a heap of noise."

"We couldn't find the door knob," explained Tess.

Bobby looked at the door. It had a spring catch on the outside, but the inside was perfectly smooth.

"Gee, I suppose you shut the door and it locked," said Bobby, who understood about doors and locks and bolts, as most boys do. "Then, of course, you couldn't open it from inside there."

"But where's the door knob?" asked Tess, and Honey Bunch stared at the door as though she would like to see the door knob, too.

"There isn't any," said Bobby. "Nothing but this catch."

"What a silly door to have!" exclaimed Tess. This wasn't very polite, but then being shut up in a dark closet might have made her forget her manners. "We don't have doors like that in our house. When you come to see us in New York, Honey Bunch, you won't get fastened in a closet without any door knob."

"No, but you can't play hide-and-seek all over the house, either," declared Bobby. "Because we live in an apartment."

Honey Bunch didn't know whether she wanted to go to see Bobby and Tess in New York or not. She was having a very good

time in her own house. But when she did
go to visit her cousins she had a good time,
too, and saw much stranger things than doors,
without door knobs. What these things were,
and what happened to Honey Bunch in the
great city of New York you'll have to read
in another book about her, to be called,
"Honey Bunch: Her First Visit to the City."
It will take a whole book to tell you, so you
may know Honey Bunch had an exciting
time.

"Stop talking about doors," said Bobby
now, very sensibly, "and come on and play.
Let's go out and play tag. It isn't a bit cold."

And we'll leave the five little cousins get-
ting ready for their game of tag, with Honey
Bunch wondering if they played tag in New
York.

THE END